River of No Return

The Twenty-Sided Sorceress: Book Nine

Annie Bellet

This book is dedicated to Matt.
Thanks for the sandwiches and unconditional love.

Soft  Paw

Softpaw raised his head to better catch the scents in the wind rolling down the valley. It was late evening and Halfheart hadn't returned to the pack. They'd had a successful hunt the day before and the pack was lazing around at the edge of the pines along the valley's base. The spring had been hotter and drier than usual and the stream here was little more than a trickle through the grey and brown rocks.

It wasn't unusual for Halfheart to wander off, especially after a hunt. Especially, Softpaw thought, since the pack had come back close to Wylde. The grey wolf had been with Softpaw's pack since the previous autumn and was still getting used to life here in the wilderness, living in the open, away from humans. Softpaw pushed away his worries with a snort and turned to look over his pack. He had a dozen wolves with him at the moment. Some, like Snowdrop and Bird, had been with him for many years, others were newer, though Halfheart was the newest at the moment.

They came to him through referrals, or sometimes just straggling into the vast wilds that made up the Frank Church River of No Return Wilderness. All of them weary of the human world, all of them broken in some way. Softpaw looked to Bird, the big red wolf resting his head on a tree root. Some, he thought, were very broken. Bird would likely never take human form again. His physical wounds had healed a century before but the mental and emotional scars remained.

The verdict was still out on Halfheart. He'd lost his mate to a horrific car accident and spiraled into an angry depression. Freyda, the Alpha of Alphas and Halfheart's pack leader, had sent him to Softpaw, worried that the wolf would lash out at humans, worried that the Council and its Justices would then come destroy him. Halfheart had picked his pack name, something that Softpaw, who was known to the human world as Aurelio, did not require, but they all did it. The name change seemed to provide separation from the pain of who they had been, of whatever had driven these wolf-shifters to the wilds and into his pack.

Softpaw worried that he had brought the pack too close to Halfheart's home town. But the Bitterroot pack always came closer to Wylde in the summer and fall. Between the presence of the druid in this part of the Frank, and the local shifters keeping bans on hunting wolves and other predators written into the law around these parts, it was safer for the pack as a whole. But perhaps not for Halfheart's broken heart.

He was dragged from his dark thoughts by Snowdrop. The white wolf emerged from the shadows of the pines and approached him with a wag of her tail. They touched noses and then she playfully bumped his shoulder with her head as she sat beside him. Softpaw reached out to her mind with his own and felt the easy connection. Snowdrop stayed with him because she loved him almost as much as she loved the wilderness. She had long ago accepted they would never be mates, for though Softpaw cared deeply for her, and though she'd been his second for over a century, and his rock through the pain of losing his daughter, there was no fire in him for her.

An impression of a grey and brown wolf ran from her mind to his with the feel of a question. Snowdrop was worried about Halfheart as well. The telepathy Softpaw was capable of wasn't strong in reverse. He could put words into the minds of his wolves, provided they let him in, but what he got back from them were more feelings, images, impressions, than true communication. Still, it was enough that shifting for human speech was unnecessary. With the longer-term members of his pack, they could get by on wolf vocalizations and body language alone much of the time.

For while his pack looked like wolves, if twice to three times the size of real wolves, they were shifters in the end and they had human impulses, instincts, and needs buried under their thick fur. Human minds that Softpaw could touch with his own.

He hadn't touched Halfheart's mind yet. Softpaw usually waited at least a couple years or until the new pack member seemed settled before doing so. He wasn't sure if he'd ever met another shifter with telepathy and his gift was not something he shared with too many. Some of the broken ones who came to his pack never learned of it. He used his instincts on whom to trust.

Snowdrop bumped his shoulder again, less gently. Softpaw growled at her but without any teeth in it and turned his head so his nose caught the scent of the wind again. There, the smell so faint he thought he'd imagined it the first time around. Wood fire with a hint of chemical to it. Not a wildfire, for there would have been more sign in the birds and insects. Which meant humans. Not far. It was time to move the pack.

"Too long," he said into Snowdrop's mind. "He's usually back before dark." The sun was a red-orange disk on the horizon, staining the grey peaks in the distance the color of raw meat.

Snowdrop lifted her head and scented the smoke, her mind feeding him worry and danger in the shape of shadowy men.

"Rouse the pack," Softpaw mind-spoke to her. "We will track our own."

Halfheart would likely have left little trail, but it didn't matter. With a heaviness settling in beside the feeling of dread in his belly, Softpaw turned his nose to the smoky wind again. His instincts were almost never wrong.

He would find his wolf in the direction of the humans. He just hoped that he wouldn't find tragedy there as well.

It was a beautiful wedding. The ceremony was held out in the woods behind where The Henhouse, Harper's mother's bed and breakfast, had stood before it was destroyed in the fight against my evil ex-boyfriend. Ezee had insisted on it, wanting to bring a good memory back to a place where we had all had so many good memories and cozy Sunday dinners together.

Before I ruined everything.

I shoved the thought away and swiped a tear from my cheek as I watched Ezee walk down the grassy path to where Iollan, the huge red-haired druid, waited. Iollan had on a great kilt woven in shades of greens and browns. His beard was trimmed and his hair hung in heavy deep red ringlets around his face, his dual colored eyes shining with love as he watched Ezee walk toward him.

Ezee wore a fitted deep purple coat that swirled around his legs, looking more like he belonged in the Matrix than in the woods. His tooled boots were shined and his hair neatly combed and oiled. They had gotten the official documents done at the County Courthouse two days before, but this was the real wedding, it was evident in my friend's eyes and on every face of the small group gathered to witness and celebrate.

Alek squeezed my hand as we watched the priest, an owl-shifter from the Nez Perce reservation who had once helped us bury Tess, begin the ceremony. Iollan held to old gods and as far as I knew Ezee held to knowledge as his religion, but they wanted to be married by someone who knew the twins. The priest had helped raise them, from what I'd gleaned during the few conversations either twin would have about their history. Two older women from the twins' tribe that Levi had introduced as cousins were present, seated in front. The rest of the attendants were myself, Alek, Brie and Ciaran, Harper and Rosie, Vivian the town vet, and of course Levi and his wife Junebug. Ezee's student and my employee Lara was there as well. She had become one of the gang over the last nine or so months. That hadn't stopped Brie from baking enough food for an army and the delicious smells from the folding tables we had set up earlier warred with the scent of forest loam, grass drying in the sun, and the warm June breeze.

"Do you, Iollan Drui, take this man, Ezekiel Chapowits, to have and to hold, to love and to cherish, in sickness and in health, for richer or poorer, for as long as you both shall live?" the priest was saying.

"They left out honor and obey," Harper stage-whispered to me from where she stood at my side.

Her mother, Rosie, must have pinched her because Harper jumped a little but quieted down.

I suppressed a grin. Ezee and Iollan, who was known around town as Yosemite because of his red hair and mysterious ways as a man of the wilds, were not really the obeying type. They made it work and I was on cloud nine that they had, despite a long, rocky start and nearly getting killed a few times.

Telling myself to stop thinking about death and destruction, I made it through the rest of the ceremony without crying too much. Then they were kissing and embracing and Alek pulled me into his arms to join in on the fun while everyone was distracted. I kind of hoped he wouldn't ask me about marriage any time soon. I wasn't sure how I felt about the institution and we hadn't seemed to need it. More paperwork now meant more to deal with in fifty or a hundred years when we were supposed to be ancient and dying, paperwork we'd have to get redone in whatever new identities we procured later.

"Food time?" Harper said, her smile big but also strained.

I pulled her in for a hug. "You okay out here, furball?" I murmured into her hair. She'd actually braided it up for the wedding, though we hadn't been able to talk her into a dress.

"Yeah," she whispered back, squeezing me tight. "It's just, I wish he were here."

"Me, too," I said, thinking of how much her brother, Max, would have loved this moment, thinking of all the happy times he was missing. "Me, too."

We managed to shrug off our melancholy thoughts and embrace the newly wedded couple.

"When are you going to walk the aisle?" Levi asked

me as we busied ourselves with cornbread, bbq ribs, and macaroni salad. He and Junebug had picked a spot across the table from Alek and me.

"Don't make me waste this delicious bread by throwing it at you," I said around a mouthful.

"We are mated," Alek said. His tone was firm, hard even, with a hint of growl to it that I found intensely sexy at the moment.

"Okay, okay, message taken," Levi said with a laugh, throwing his hands up in surrender.

"Married people want everyone else to follow them," Harper said as she set her loaded plate down next to mine.

"You'd have to get a date first," Levi said. Then he froze as he clearly realized what an asshole he sounded like. "Shit. Sorry. I'll just shut up. Look at this delicious bread!"

Harper stuck her tongue out at him. "When I find someone who turns my crank, I'll let you know. Actually, I won't. I'll be too busy cranking." She waggled her brows. "Sadly Jade stole the only person around here with manners, so it might be a while."

"She certainly is a thief." Alek laid an arm around my shoulders as I snuck a rib off his plate.

Grinning, I sucked the meat off my stolen rib with exaggerated glee. It was good to be out in the sunlight, no one trying to kill us, my friends all here and celebrating life. I hoped it lasted.

Harper's mother, Rosie, had come back a month after Harper had returned. She had bought the house formerly owned by Peggy the librarian, a witch murdered by my evil ex. The town hadn't been able to come to agreement on what to do with the property so when Rose, a long-time town member, offered to take it from them, they sold it for a song. She had torn the guts out of the house and remodeled it, no mean feat in an Idaho winter, and was living comfortably in town. Neither Rose nor Harper had said a word about what was to become of the Henhouse property. I assumed there were too many bad memories now that Max was dead.

"Is it time for speeches yet?" Rosie said, rising from her camp chair. Unlike her daughter, Rosie had worn a soft blue dress and a string of pearls. She smiled as she pulled a folder of papers out of the large embroidered canvas bag she used as a purse.

"It isn't so much a speech," she said as she walked around the tables to where Ezee and Iollan sat, "as a gift. But I want to say something before you open it."

Ezee took the papers from her and nodded, looking at a loss for words.

"I have lived on this land since before it adjoined a national park," Rosie stated, surprising me. Shifters and other long-lived people tended not to talk about age and time much if they could help it. "But life changes, those we love come and go. Change is one of the only givens in this world and we can let it help us like the snake shedding its skin on the rocks, or we can cling to what has gone. This land brought me joy, it brought me family, and it has brought me sorrow and pain. The up and the down of the wheel as it turns. Sky and Earth."

She spread her hands wide and swept them up before turning back to directly address Ezee and Iollan.

"Ezekiel, you are a creature of modern comfort and the modern world. Iollan, you are a creature of the wilds and the wood. This land stands between both, a place on the edge of wilderness and civilization. Take it as my gift. Find joy here. Build your family, however they may come to you. Plow my sorrows and my joys under so that you may grow your own life here."

Fuck it, I was crying again and this time the

waterworks didn't want to turn off no matter how hard I blinked. Looking around I wasn't the only one who felt like someone had dumped a truckload of chopped onions into our laps. Even Alek's eyes were bright, though he wasn't quite shedding tears yet.

Ezee leapt over the table with shifter grace and caught Rosie up in a hug. "We will," he said, his voice ringing in the early summer air. "You are our family, too, and all our joy is here already." He looked past Rosie's head to Harper and she nodded vigorously through her tears. Her hand reached for mine under the table, however.

I laced my fingers through hers and leaned toward her.

"Shit, I only got them a KitchenAid mixer," I muttered.

Harpers laugh broke through her tears and she squeezed my hand before she let go.

We'd made it nearly a year without a single supernatural incident or anyone trying to kill me. I couldn't help but think about it as Alek drove us back to our apartment over my store, Pwned Comics and Games. I always seemed to start fearing another shoe dropping whenever things got too calm or too happy lately. To be fair to my paranoia, that shoe usually did fall sooner or later.

I had made sure to keep up my magical training as well as the physical training with Alek. I wasn't going to be leaping buildings in a single bound without magical assistance anytime soon, but I could run a few miles without wanting to fall over and never move again, and Alek said my punches almost stung, which from him was big praise.

I pushed away my dark thoughts and instead thought about Ezee and Iollan, who were spending their honeymoon at some forest retreat with a natural hot spring. There was no room service, but Iollan had promised Ezee it was well equipped and beautiful. I hoped they had a peaceful and relaxing two weeks away. Someone around this place should get a vacation every once and a while. And when they came back, we could start planning their new home. Levi had already offered to start calling architects while Ezee was on his honeymoon. My whole group was excited for this new start and it was hard, even with my paranoid moods, not to want to engage in their enthusiasm.

"That car has been behind us since we pulled onto the main road," Alek said. His eyes flicked to the rearview mirror and then to me as he kept driving.

I ignored the gooseflesh on my arms. "There's only one road into town from here," I said. The car was just headlights in the side mirror.

I let magic fill my blood and wrapped the truck in a bubble of invisible shielding force, just in case. It would be tiring to maintain all the way into town but better safe than riddled with bullets, I figured.

We sat in silence as the lights of Wylde appeared, Alek tense next to me, and I trying to relax and hold the shield with minimal use of magic. The car turned off at the gas station next to the Lutheran church. My breath gasped out as I released the magic with a half sigh, half giggle.

"We are not made for quiet lives," Alek said with a rueful laugh as he stopped crushing the steering wheel. There were dents where his fingers had dug in.

"I could get used to it," I said, hoping that was true. I rubbed my twenty-sided die talisman, feeling the hard bump of Samir's heart where it rested like a tiny ruby in the one-spot on the die.

Nearly two years since I stabbed him with the Alpha and Omega, effectively ending his life, though until another sorcerer swallowed his heart, Samir would be only mostly dead. I hadn't told my friends yet. I meant to, but there was never a good moment to do so, never the right time. I feared what they would say, Harper most of all. She had lost so much because of Samir. I felt it was kinder to let him be dead enough. I wasn't sure they would understand that I couldn't eat his heart for so many reasons.

I didn't want his power. I didn't want his ghost living in my mind. I didn't want to know his history, to feel the lives of all the sorcerers and magic users and who knew who else he'd murdered over the years.

Oh, and that little detail about killing him would apparently break some ancient seal and allow a lot of magic and powerful not-so-nice critters back into the world. I had no desire to cause an apocalypse, even a slow magical one.

So Samir would stay a ruby gem in my talisman and I would hope that what I hadn't told my friends wouldn't hurt me. Or them.

We pulled into the back parking lot behind my building. It was late, Brie and Ciaran and my shop had been closed for the wedding, so I didn't expect any vehicles besides the Brie's Bakery delivery truck.

The lot wasn't empty. A black Mercedes was parked in one of the spaces directly behind my apartment. A white man wearing a suit stood leaning against the driver's side door. He was in his forties with short dark hair and gave a little wave as we drove into the lot, making no mistake possible that he wasn't waiting for me. He looked unarmed and I could see both his hands, but still. Men in suits with nice cars never came bearing large checks or chocolate in my experience.

Alek pulled the truck in and then reached across me to open the glove box. He got his gun out as I let magic fill my blood once more.

"You all right?" Alek murmured.

"Let's do this," I said. I had to admit, as I got out of the truck with magic humming in my veins, I kind of hoped the guy was trouble. Just a little. Easy trouble. A small shoe.

Turned out, he was a lawyer and the shoe dropping fit in an envelope.

The lawyer, who introduced himself as Mr. Allen, insisted that we go inside. Alek made no pretense of hiding his gun as we walked up the stairs to the apartment. The man seemed human enough and wasn't carrying any obvious weapons, nor did he set off my wards, so we ended up sitting on opposite sides of my kitchen table. Alek loomed over me like a celebrity's bodyguard. Or maybe like a supervillain's henchman. I imagined Mr. Allen was thinking more along the latter lines from the sweat that beaded on his forehead as he drew a small blue envelope and a folder from his briefcase.

"I was hired by Samir Sampson," he said. I carefully

kept my face neutral and my hands on the table. "There were instructions left with my firm that if we did not hear from Mr. Sampson within a certain time period that we were to find you, Ms. Crow, and deliver this." He tapped the blue envelope.

"I don't want it," I said. "Whatever that is, I don't care. Samir and I are old business. You can find him and tell him you tried and I said no. I'm good." I reminded myself to refer to Samir in present tense like he was out there somewhere, living his life, rather than a ruby droplet hung around my neck.

Because wearing the magically shrunken hearts of my enemies wasn't a supervillain thing to do at all. Hmm. I pushed that thought away. After all, Samir had used the alias Samson so who exactly was the histrionic bro there, right?

"Please," Mr. Allen said. He glanced up at Alek and a muscle in his jaw twitched. "This is our duty. I don't care if you throw this into the trash after I leave, but please sign here and initial here, and then I will leave."

He pushed papers he had taken from the folder toward me. His dark eyes were earnest. Just a man doing his job.

"What exactly were your instructions?" I asked.

"If we had not heard from our client after a certain period of time, we were to find you, Jade Crow, and deliver this envelope. In person. He was very specific about that. He also said that if delivery was triggered by circumstances, you would know what this was."

Mr. Allen gave me a nervous smile that I imagined had more to do with Alek standing like a six-foot-six murder machine over my shoulder than with me. I was still wearing a freaking sundress and silver strappy sandals, for frak's sake. I'd even put on lipstick for the wedding. I was the least intimidating I ever looked, except maybe after a forty-eight hour new expansion World of Warcraft binge with my friends.

I took a deep breath. Let it out. Then I picked up the heavy and probably expensive pen Mr. Allen had laid out and scanned the documents. It was a bunch of legalese releasing the law firm from its duty, saying I acknowledged receipt, and all that stuff that if a normal person wrote it would take half a paragraph but lawyers bill by the hour so I guess they needed extra words. I signed.

"Great," I said. "Done. Have a good night, Mr. Allen."

I kept the pen and he didn't say a word about it as he packed up his things and scurried out the door and down the steps. I stood on the landing and watched him drive away.

"You going to open it?" Alek asked me.

"I'm going to bring it down into the parking lot and incinerate it with mage fire until I create a new pothole." I leaned back into his warm bulk with a sigh.

"Before opening it?" he said. His voice was a low rumble against my back and his warm breath tickled my ear as he nuzzled my hair, messing up the intricate braids that had taken hours to do.

"Curiosity killed the cat," I muttered, pulling away from him.

"Satisfaction brought it back," he said.

"That's usually my line." I mock-glared up at him.

He stepped aside and gestured at the small blue envelope.

It hadn't set off my wards, but that didn't make whatever was in there not a trap. Samir had specialized in magical items, especially ones that hurt people or exploded or controlled those around him. I summoned my magic again, using my home brewed version of Mage Hand to lift the envelope. I backed down the stairs and out into the now empty lot, the envelope floating with me.

Holding my hands as though I were gripping it, I ripped the envelope in half with my mind. A small metal object fell out and was caught by my magic, hanging suspended in the air. A key. I pulled it toward me for a better look.

The key was about the length of my thumb and old fashioned in a skeleton key style. The handle part ended in a stylized heart with scroll bits on it. The key part was a rectangle shape with an S carved out of the middle of it. I had no idea what this key went to and had never seen a key quite like it, nor a door or other object I could imagine using it on. There was no magic on or in the key that I could determine. It lacked any of the sweet scent of Samir's magic.

"A key," Alek said helpfully as he walked up to me.

"Yeah. Just a normal-ass normal ancient looking key from a dude who spent my life trying to kill me or become a god. No magic I can feel," I added.

"Never seen it before?" Alek said. His tone put his question as more of a statement. He could read me like his favorite book.

I shrugged. "Nope. I think Samir thought I'd know what this was because I think he assumed if he disappeared it was on the tiny chance I kicked his ass and ate him. But without his memories, no way to know."

"He assumed you would do what he would do." Alek chuckled.

"He was an ass," I said. I wasn't sure why he found this situation funny.

"You going to destroy it?"

I looked at the key still floating in front of us and I couldn't stop my own giggles from rising. Okay, it was a little funny. There we were, treating this non-magical key like it was plutonium. Samir had probably just sent it to fuck with me because he couldn't resist that shit.

But... there was the little voice in my head that sounded a lot like Ghost-Tess, warning me that Samir always played the long game and he always played to win.

"No," I said. "There's always a chance it's a warning of something worse to come and then I'll be like 'shit, guys, I destroyed the MacGuffin that can save the world' and everyone will be like you are the worst hero ever."

"What is this MacGuffin?" Alek said, an adorably confused look on his face.

I snatched the key out of the air, went to put it in

my pocket, realized I was still wearing a damn dress with no pockets, and instead held it awkwardly.

"I'll tell you inside. I want to put this in my warded box, then I can explain movie tropes." I started walking back to the apartment. I hoped this would be the end of it, but I had a feeling this was just the beginning.

Alek

Alek knew something was wrong before the sheriff, Rachel Lee, had to say a word. The wolf-shifter's stocky body radiated tension as Alek walked up to where she was waiting by her official vehicle. He had picked up two coffees on his way. Rachel took one with a nod.

"Trouble?" Alek said. It was only half a question.

"Freyda called on one of their burner lines," Rachel said. She started walking around to the driver's side. "Get in."

Coffee cups safely stowed in their holders, Rachel peeled out of the lot and turned the wrong way if they were headed to the Den. Alek waited patiently for her to tell him the rest. She liked to think things through and often got lost in her thoughts as she puzzled over details.

"She wouldn't say much on the phone, but it sounds like she's been threatened," Rachel said after a minute. "We're meeting her at the old Hilltop diner off the highway."

"Trap?" Alek asked, wondering what could have spooked the Alpha of Alphas, the strongest wolf-shifter around. Freyda was not one to scare easily. If someone had threatened her and she was calling in their help, it was likely very serious.

"No, don't think so," Rachel said. She gripped the steering wheel as though it were the neck of someone she was thinking about killing.

Her scent said fear, her tension said anger. It was not a mix that Alek liked, and the circumstances did not seem to warrant it. There was something she was not telling him yet. Alek did not realize he was growling until Rachel glanced at him and made a face.

"She said it was related to the Council of Nine," she said with a small huff of breath.

A chill crawled down Alek's spine. He sat up straighter and took a deep breath, staring out at the road ahead. He had told Rachel the gist of what had happened with the Council, what little he knew. The Council was broken, at least one of its members succumbing to madness and instigating the murder of one other of the Nine. It had been nearly two years since he had last dealt with the Council.

Almost as long since he had last heard from any of his former Justice friends, either.

They made the rest of the drive in silence. The diner looked deserted as they pulled into the empty gravel parking lot. The Hilltop had been vacant at least as long as Alek had been in Wylde. A new on and off ramp had been built about two miles farther up the highway, more convenient for hitting the main road into town, and for Juniper College which provided much of the town business and funding. The diner location was no longer prime for weary travelers making their way along the edge of the Frank wilderness. Nobody wanted it, so it stood boarded up and empty, a paint-chipped relic of a different time.

Alek got out cautiously, one hand resting on his hip near his gun. The air smelled of car exhaust and the dust Rachel's SUV had kicked up on turning into the parking lot. There had been no rain for five days as summer had decided to get a head start. He picked up only Rachel's scent, no other wolves.

"Maybe we beat her here?" Rachel said. She had her gun out but her finger was off the trigger and the weapon pointed at the ground. Still, she was ready for trouble.

Alek took his cue from her and pulled his own gun. He raised an eyebrow at Rachel's unspoken question. They both knew that Freyda was not the type to be late to a meeting.

"I'll go left, you go right," Rachel said. She did not wait for his answer but moved off around the side of the square, green building.

Alek went right. Grass and weeds were reclaiming the parking lot and making forays through cracks in the cement slab around the diner. The gutters sagged with old needles from the scraggly pines shading the back side of the building. The boards were unmolested, the chain on the side door he passed looked intact. His skin still crawled with the feeling of being watched and he could not let go of the tension that told him something was off.

Behind the diner was a half-toppled wire fence. The pine trees and the scrub brush beneath them had taken over this area. The ground here had never been paved, just gravel, and nature had reclaimed it with a vengeance.

The breeze changed direction, rustling through the trees and bringing the scent of another wolf-shifter to Alek's nose. The scent was mingled with the smell of ashes, as though from a campfire and he could not pick out if it were a wolf he knew or had scented before. He raised his gun and pointed it at the brush in front of him even though his keen vision still saw nothing in the shifting shadows of the branches. He heard more than saw Rachel moving up on his side.

"Come out," Alek said.

Now the brush rustled in a way that was distinct from the breeze. A large, lanky grey wolf with streaks of brown in her fur emerged, grey eyes focused on him. Then she looked to Rachel.

Alek lowered his gun, some of the tension draining out. Freyda.

"You okay?" Rachel said as Freyda shifted.

Freyda shook her head. Her breathing was labored as though she had sprinted and sweat streaked her clothing.

"You came on foot?" Alek asked. From her human

body's appearance, she had come at least some of the way on two legs. Which made sense, given how exposed the roads were on this side of town.

"I ran here from the Den. It wasn't safe to take a vehicle," Freyda said. She lifted her head and flared her nostrils, her mouth slightly open as she smelled the air.

"We're alone here," Rachel said.

"And too exposed," Alek said, looking around. The trees and the elevation of the highway kept them out of view of the cars and trucks he could hear occasionally passing, but the diner was exposed to the road that ran parallel to the highway all the way down to the other on-ramp about three miles away. There would be some traffic on this road from the people who lived out that way though only a few homes dotted the landscape here.

"I'll pull the truck around, you two get that back door open. Nobody will see my vehicle from the road and we can talk inside," Rachel said after a moment as Freyda kept looking around and did not seem about to start explaining herself.

"Breaking and entering?" Alek said, putting his gun away.

"It'll give me an excuse to have been out here,"

Rachel said, flashing him a grin. "We can write up a report afterward."

Alek easily broke the lock on the back door. He moved into the dim interior, his nose telling him no one had been in here for a long time. The place had been cleaned but there was still a hint of grease and humanity clinging stubbornly to the surfaces of the kitchen. He doubted there was power but tried a switch anyway. Nothing.

Rachel brought a Coleman lantern in with her and pulled the door shut. The lamp was plenty of light for the three shifters to see by. They made their way into the diner proper. The booths had all been sold off or stolen except for one that stood lonely in a corner, half-pulled out of its place.

Freyda brushed at the dust, gave up on it, and sat. Alek remained standing, but Rachel took up a place across from the Alpha.

"I'm sorry," Freyda said. "I had to be sure I was not seen and that you were not followed." Her eyes flicked to Alek and her mouth pressed into a tight line.

"We weren't followed," Rachel said. No cars had been behind them once they had left town and they had only seen two vehicles coming the other way.

"I'm being watched," Freyda said. "We drove them off but I can feel that they are out there."

"Freyda," Alek said, trying to keep the growl out of his voice. "Who?"

"The Council," she said, her spooked eyes settling on him finally.

Alek snarled before he controlled himself as both wolves leaned away from him.

"The Council is broken," he said.

"I should start at the beginning," Freyda said. "Alek, sit, please. I can't take you looming right now."

Alek suppressed the smile that twitched his lips. Jade hated him looming over her most of the time, too. He wished his mate were here, although her usual way of solving everything with fire would perhaps not work so well in this instance. Yet.

If the remnants of the Council were here, Alek had a feeling it would eventually come to a fight. It had in New Orleans and he doubted the situation had improved during the years after.

Once he had settled himself on the edge of the bench next to Rachel, his long legs stretched out to the side, Freyda began her story.

"Late last night four wolves showed up at the Den.

They asked to speak to the Alpha of Alphas and said it was urgent. They told me they were from someone they called The First," she said.

Alek felt another growl in his chest. The First was the first shifter granted powers by the Fates. He had never met the Council, but he knew that the First controlled the Emissary, a powerful spirit bound to the Council to guide their visions and speak to Justices through dreams.

"Go on," he said, as Freyda paused and drew a small swirl in the dust on the table with nervous fingers.

"I did not believe them. I knew the Council was broken. Then they howled and forced us all to shift, just as you did. But they were in still in their human forms." Freyda's gaze was locked on Alek's own. "Worse than that, their howls turned us submissive, every last damn one of us. It was like a crushing wave of fear, Alek. I've never felt the like. All I wanted to do was roll on my belly and beg for mercy. I barely fought it off and managed to bite the leg of the wolf who walked too close. That seemed to break their concentration and I was able to control my pack again, but they had made their point and backed off."

"What did they want?" Alek said. The power she

described was Justice power, only more than he had ever had. There had been no fear component to his ability to force another shifter to change shape.

"They said things are changing. That the time for shifters to live in the shadows is coming to an end." She shivered and Alek felt Rachel stiffen beside him. He imagined it was difficult to look at someone as strong as Freyda, the Alpha of Alphas, and see such fear. Not reassuring for his wolf friend.

"The humans will slaughter us again," Rachel said. "Have they all gone mad?"

"They have," Alek said. His heart felt like it weighed a thousand pounds. The old ways were lost, the Council truly broken. Even now, huddled in secret over a dusty table illuminated only by a small electric lamp, Alek did not want to accept that truth. His gods had become monsters.

"They said I must accept the will of the First, or we will be eliminated. I drove them off, but this morning they were there, lurking on the edge of our property. They did not try the howling again, though I had all of us put in ear plugs before confronting them. We drove them off with guns this time, but I fear it will not last. I fear they are still there, watching," Freyda said. "That's why I came on my own, that's why I ran here. I worry they will come for those unprotected in town."

"No one is unprotected," Alek said and Rachel echoed him.

"They came to you because you are the Alpha of Alphas and they likely want to turn you to make getting the other packs in line more simple. Plus we have a great many shifters here," Rachel said.

"They have Justice powers," Freyda said. She ran a dusty hand through her short, wheat-colored hair. "If they bring more people next time or start picking us off…"

"This will not happen," Alek said. He folded his arms, knowing he would do whatever it took to wipe the fear from the Alpha's pale face. "You resisted them, broke their power. Drove them off, yes?"

Freyda's gaze returned to him and she nodded, sitting up straighter. "I did. Then I ran here in the shadows like a coward," she said, frowning.

"No, that was good," Rachel said. "If they are watching you, it's best to keep your movements and your exact allies secret until we can find these four and get rid of them."

"More will come," Freyda said. "That's what they made it sound like. Join us or be destroyed in the coming war, that's what they said. I don't want war. Not with shifters, not with humans. My father created the Peace to prevent it. Justices were supposed to prevent it."

"War will not come," Alek said, wishing he felt as confident as he sounded. His whole life had been dedicated to keeping shifters secret, to preserving the peace with humans and keeping his people safe. He had sacrificed almost everything for that end. He had killed so many. He shook his head to clear his dark thoughts.

"If it does," Rachel said, "we'll be ready. But first we'll warn everyone. Get every shifter in this town looking out for them."

"I sent a wolf into the Frank to find Softpaw," Freyda said. "His pack is strong and he's never been one to shy away from a fight if needed."

"Good," Alek said. "I will talk to Jade. Perhaps we can find these wolves and I can have my own talk with them." From the look on Freyda's face, his smile was not pleasant.

They rose by unspoken agreement and made their

way out of the diner, all three pausing to listen for a moment at the door before moving through. No sounds beyond a car speeding through on the highway and the shifting branches of the pines dropping the occasional needle onto the metal roof.

"I left my pack with instructions to shoot anyone they didn't recognize, so I had better get back," Freyda said, sniffing the air as they moved into the sunlight, blinking.

"We'll drop you off up the highway so you don't have to run as far," Rachel said. "Then we can swing back and do a report on this break-in." She grinned up at Alek as she motioned to where he had smashed the lock. "Too bad we'll never catch the miscreants who did this."

"And this used to be such a nice town," Freyda said with a wry smile as Alek shrugged.

He took a moment as the women moved to the SUV to breathe deep and collect his thoughts. He had been waiting for fallout from the Council breaking. The Nazi wolf brothers who had come after him the year before were just the beginning of the trouble he was expecting. Now it seemed the rest of the wave would break soon.

"Alek?" Rachel called out. She and Freyda had paused at the bumper, both looking back at him.

Their appearances were very different, Freyda tall and lanky with pale freckled skin and light hair, Rachel short and stocky with light brown skin, dark eyes, and black hair, but they mirrored each other's stance as perfectly as professional dancers might mirror a partner. Alek shook his head.

"Wolves," he said. "I am sick of wolves, present company excepted."

After he climbed into the front seat, Alek found his coffee had gone cold. With a sigh he accepted that this was likely only the beginning of a very bad day.

3

"Want lunch?" Lara offered as I finished unboxing this week's comic book order.

"You going for sandwiches?" I asked. I straightened up, rubbing my lower back. Now to sort the comics into the reserve cubbies for my regulars and then figure out what to put where on the new-release shelf. A fresh week was always work, but also fun. I got the read all the new stuff first.

"Yeah, got a paper to finish tonight so I could use a meatball hoagie."

"Sounds good to me." I dug cash out of my wallet and held out a ten-dollar bill to my assistant.

"Nah, I got this." Lara waved off my money.

"Angling for employee of the month?" I asked, grinning. Lara was my only employee.

"I expect a trophy any day now. No speeches though," she said, returning my grin. "Want the usual?"

"Sure."

I was nothing if not predictable about my food orders and Lara had been working for me long enough that she could probably recite by heart everything I ordered from any of the places around. I didn't order out every day, of course, since I could just walk upstairs and eat a sandwich or leftovers out of my own fridge. Still, I never turned down food someone else cooked. There had been so many times in my life where affording a meal out was a foreign concept that I still got a small thrill out of knowing I could.

The early afternoon was quiet and no one came into the store as I sorted comics. A delivery truck pulled up before Lara was back, which confused me since the shipment I'd been expecting had already arrived for the day. I watched curiously out the front windows as two men wrestled a large rectangular package down from the truck.

The package looked more like something Ciaran, my leprechaun antique-dealing neighbor, would order, but the men hauled it up to my door and pushed inside.

"Jade Crow?" One of them asked. Sweat beaded his pale forehead.

"That's me," I said. "Not sure what that is, though." I motioned to the large package they had hauled into the open space in front of the dice display counter.

"Got your name on it," the man said with a shrug.

My wards hadn't pinged me so I returned his shrug. "Sometimes these game companies like to send promo stuff," I guessed.

"Whatever, sign here," the guy said. Customer service was clearly not his strong suit. His companion grinned apologetically at me as I scribbled my name on the tablet he held out.

I waited until the men had left and then pulled a knife out of a drawer under the cash register. There was no return address on the package or listed sender, which I thought was weird. My name and the store address were printed on a sheet of paper and taped down. The package had been shipped from New York, judging by the postage markers.

After a momentary debate for if I should wait for Lara to return, I cut the box open. It was probably some kind of promo thing which would get recycled or buried in the back storage area or given away to one of my friends or customers. The box was full of packing peanuts. I made a face, wishing anyone who used this much of the static-clinging, mess-making Styrofoam an express trip to a special hell.

Shoving aside some of the peanuts, which of course started flowing out of the box and onto my clean floor, I spied ornately carved dark wood and a large metal handle with a keyhole above it. The handle had been cast to look like a tree branch. Someone had mailed me a door.

I thought of the key upstairs and a chill crawled up my spine. As though it had been blocked by the packing materials, the cold, sweet scent of magic floated up to me as I bent over the box.

Samir's magic.

I was halfway out the shop door before I controlled myself. My heart punched my rib cage as I grabbed my D20 talisman and checked for the millionth time that Samir's heart was still there, embedded in its divot on the one spot on the die. I summoned magic, then realized that trying to destroy the package might have dire consequences for my shop, I turned the spell from

ANNIE BELLET

fire to warding. My eyes caught the salt and pepper shakers I had behind the counter for those days when we took lunch out on the back lot in the little picnic area I'd set up there.

Grabbing in the salt, I tore it open and used it in combination with my power to build a circle around the entire package. The thin white line glowed faintly purple with my power and the scent of Samir's magic cut off as I closed the spell. Sweat trickled down my spine as I forced myself to breathe again.

The door chimed as Lara returned. She stopped a few steps inside the store, the bag of sandwiches hanging from one hand as she took in the scene. Her brown eyes flicked from me, who was leaning against the dice counter looking like I'd just tried to run a marathon, all sweating and out of breath, to the faintly glowing salt circle around a large, half-opened box.

"I knew it," she said. "I knew packing peanuts were evil!"

"Not that," I managed to gasp as my mind raced to figure out how to explain. Lara knew some of my past and she knew there had been a big showdown with another sorcerer, though she hadn't been in Wylde then.

44

"The package is also evil?" she guessed.

"It's a door," I said. "I think. A magic door. Made by my evil ex."

"So the door is evil? Is it going to blow up before I get to eat my sandwich?"

I shook my head. "Most employees would be handing in notice at this point," I said.

"Nah, they'd have exited after your mate got shot in the neck outside, so it's lucky you have me instead," Lara said. "But seriously, should we do something about that thing before we eat? I don't recall ordering a side of 'uncertain fate' with my lunch."

Alek had been shot the summer before and Lara had taken it all in stride in much the same way. I really wondered if there was more to her life before coming to Juniper College than she talked about. She had family members who were in emergency health care, so maybe it was just that. I'd never met someone so even-keeled and in that moment never had I been so grateful for it. Her being so calm helped me calm down.

"I have a ward around it," I said. "I don't even know if it is truly dangerous, it's just an instinctive reaction, I guess." I decided not to mention the key delivered via lawyer express the night before. I had no answers for anyone, so what was the point?

"This is going to be fun to explain to our patrons," Lara said as she made her way around the package, careful not to disturb the glowing salt circle.

"Um, yeah," I said. She had a point. I needed to find another solution. "Let's eat, and then I'll think of somewhere more permanent to stash this."

Lara pointed out that the delivery people had been fine and so probably just reboxing the door and putting it somewhere would be fairly safe. In the end we got it moved to the back storage area, partially due to Lara's awesome shifter strength. I fixed another ward around it just in case. It wasn't a permanent solution, but until I knew what the door was and what it did, it was the best I could do short of taking it out back and burning it. Which had appeal, but part of me couldn't resist the mystery.

Even gone, Samir still had his hooks in me, and was still playing his stupid games.

Which reminded me again of the damn key. The mystery key. And now a mystery door.

"Fuck you," I muttered as we closed up the storage room. I found myself rubbing the hard gem of Samir's heart with my thumb. "I'm not playing your games today."

"You okay?" Lara asked, turning back.

"I'm okay," I said, hoping it was true. "I just hate how sometimes the past feels like quicksand."

Samir was gone, but still he pulled me down. I smiled at Lara and went to clean up the stray packing peanuts. Life went on, no matter how treacherous my footing.

Alek

The problem with being a sheriff in a small town like Wylde was that it could be hard to go anywhere without someone waving Rachel down and needing to complain or ask about something. Alek sat quietly through those situations and by now most denizens of the town did not seem to wonder too much about the big, silent blond who rode around with Sheriff Lee some of the time.

When a middle-aged human male in a camo jacket with the sleeves cut off and riding an ATV down the back road near the Hilltop diner flagged the sheriff down, Alek sighed with a mix of impatience and amusement.

"That's the oldest of Bertha Dogget's boys, I forget his damn name though," Rachel said. "Give me a minute."

Alek shrugged. Rachel stopped her vehicle and rolled down the window. Road grit and human sweat mingled with diesel assaulted Alek's nose.

"Hey there," the man said, squinting in the sunlight. "What brings you out our way, Sheriff?"

"Broken chain on the old diner," Rachel said. "Nothing looks messed with. Probably just some jokers drinking too much last weekend. Can I help you, Mr. Dogget?"

"It's not a big deal," he said, running a hand through thinning brown hair. "Just that Hank's been trimming the trees between our property with his shotgun again and it bothers the dogs. Rains some buckshot onto the kennels and that gets mom all riled, ya'know? I would've tried talking to him myself but you know ol' Hank."

Rachel chuckled. Alek suppressed his own amusement. Even he knew of the old man who lived alone out this way. There was probably a call a week about him shooting at cars or ranting in the middle of the night about spirits taking over his barn or someone threatening his roosters. Half the calls came from Hank himself. He tended to shoot at people approaching his property, even his neighbors, but had a strange respect for law enforcement, so Rachel or her deputies were always flipping coins to see who had to deal with him that week.

"I'll talk to him," Rachel said. "And thanks for letting us know about the Hilltop diner."

The man nodded then looked confused. "The diner?"

"The chain being broken?" Rachel said gently. "We checked it out and we'll send someone to relock it up, no worries at all."

"Oh yeah, of course, always happy to help. Thanks, Sheriff. Have a good day." The man smiled bemusedly as Rachel rolled up her window.

Alek looked at Rachel with a small shake of his head. She'd been sheriff for a while now and he was constantly amazed at the juggling act she performed to keep Wylde's supernatural community hidden and its human community safe and more or less content. She had just smoothly talked a man into believing he had made a report, which could conveniently cover their own presence and fill out the missing details in the paperwork.

"I'm going to send a deputy to drive past the Den," Rachel said, her face sliding from smile to serious as they headed back to town. "See if he notices anything odd. I'll just tell him we've had reports of someone illegally burning trash out that way."

"Make sure he does not engage," Alek said. If the Council, or what remained of it, was threatening the Alpha of Alphas, there was no longer a guarantee they would keep violence against humans at a minimum. The rules that had guided his whole life as a Justice were gone and until he could determine what game the broken council was playing, no one knew what the new rules were.

"I'll tell him to just drive by and report any vehicles or people. No engagement," Rachel said. She gave Alek an annoyed glance.

"Apologies," he said with a slight dip of his head. "I know you know your job. That was smoothly done back there."

Rachel harrumphed but her lips curved into a smile as she put her attention back on the road.

"You want to loop Jade in? We could swing by the store."

Alek stared at the passing trees for a moment. "Not yet," he said. "Let us see what your deputy sees or does not see first."

Jade would start worrying as soon as she was told and likely want to go solve the problem herself in grand magical fashion. Alek grinned as he thought of his mate. Whatever the problem with the Council, he had a feeling they would not be prepared for Jade.

But though things had been quiet, Jade had been on edge ever since he had been shot the previous summer. Samir sending her a strange key had done nothing for her mood. While Alek wanted her happy, he did not want her in danger for no reason, especially when he could not be sure what the danger was. Just because she itched for something she could fight did not mean he could let her go into trouble without all the information yet.

And there was still a small part of him that felt the Council was his problem, his mess to clean up or help resolve, somehow. A shifter problem. He would utilize all his allies if he had to, his mate included, but not until he knew something solid about the situation. He had walked blind into one trap already with the Council and nearly lost both his mentor and his own life.

This time he would employ more caution. This time he would be ready.

"Hey, stranger," I said to Alek.

It was late afternoon and I hadn't heard from him all day. No call to say he was missing lunch. A "something came up" text was it in response to my very definitely not clingy girlfriend text. Singular. I had only sent him one, right after the fiasco with the door, not wanting to alarm him.

"Hi." He ran a distracted hand through shoulder-length white-blond hair that had been in a ponytail that morning but clearly fallen to the mercy of his nerves at some point during the afternoon. His face gave away little but from the tense set of his shoulders and the repressed energy in his movements, I knew

Alek was unhappy about something.

"I'm taking off," Lara said with a glance between us. Shifters are better at reading body language than I am and her reaction to Alek's appearance told me that I'd been dead on. "See you tomorrow." She grabbed her backpack and was out the door before I could frame a response, leaving Alek and I alone in my shop.

I stepped right into Alek's personal zone and pressed my fingers against his sweat-damp chest. I had to tip my head back to look into his face but the small smile I got was worth it.

"You first or me?" I asked.

"I have nothing," Alek said with a sigh. "Just possible trouble."

"No warm bodies to make scream and bleed?" I guessed.

Alek's reluctant smile turned into a toothy grin that would have scared the shit out of anyone who wasn't totally sure of his feelings for them. Not me though. I'm a big girl without weak knees or a sudden desire to flee the tiger. Yep.

"No bodies. Possible trouble with a former Council member," he said.

Motioning to the chairs by the war gaming demo

table, I followed him and we sat where we had a good view of the door in case anyone came in to get their Pokemon card fix. He filled me in quickly on the details of his day.

"The deputy we sent out to check around the Den saw nothing, so we did our own drive past. Neither of us could sense much. Lingering scent of wolf we did not recognize. Tire tracks that might be from anyone. Freyda is keeping everyone close now."

"Freyda is freaked out?" I said when he was done. I tried to imagine the tall, strong Alpha wolf scared of anything. She'd faced down a murderous former Justice and a bomb without blinking.

"We do not like being helpless," Alek said in Russian. His ice-blue eyes stared into the middle distance and whatever he saw in his mind's eye made his shoulders hunch.

"Hey." I took one of his hands in mine, rubbing my thumbs over his warm palm. "Whatever trouble might come up, I got your back. We've dealt with everything thrown at us so far. Freyda isn't alone. Neither are you."

His gaze came back to mine and his smile returned. "I know," he said switching back to English. "I hate waiting without knowing full danger or having a good plan for it."

"That's two of us," I muttered, thinking about the damn door.

"Your day was good?" Alek asked?

"I got a delivery from Samir."

Alek's head tipped slightly to the side and he raised an eyebrow, waiting for me to explain.

"A door. A big fucking magic door that I have no idea what to do with." I realized I'd let go of his hand and was clutching my D20 talisman, my thumb pressed to the hard nub of Samir's heart gem.

"Is it dangerous?"

I let go of the talisman with effort. "No idea. I put it under ward in the storeroom."

"Then it will keep while we get dinner," Alek said. He rose. "Steak?"

"I have to keep the shop open for three more hours. That whole working for a living thing?"

Alek looked around pointedly at the empty shop. It was not likely to be a busy night. Harper would probably come by. Levi probably wouldn't since he was spending some quality time with his wife while his brother was on his honeymoon. Game was suspended for the moment and no new expansions had come out this month yet for any of our current favorites.

"Very subtle," I said, rolling my eyes at him. "My boss will let me off this once, I guess." I thought about pantomiming asking myself for permission, but from Alek's expression he was still tired, frustrated, and probably hungry. Snark would not placate a hungry tiger.

I grabbed my keys from under the counter. I dashed off a quick note saying we were closed early tonight and would open again normal hours the following day. Joy of a small town, people expected that kind of notice or they'd probably call the police worrying I was being murdered in here or something. I stuck the note to the door, flipped the sign to "closed" and locked up.

"I'm all yours, tiger," I said.

A cool shower, a very sweaty "let's help each other forget all our cares" session, another cool shower, and a plate of grilled meat later, I felt like I could conquer the world. Samir's games aside, he was stuck in my necklace and I was living my life to its fucking fullest.

We had just put on the new King Arthur movie when Alek reached for the controller and paused it, his head cocked.

"People coming?" I asked. I felt the familiar thrum of my magic as I let it flow into me. I was really itching for a fight and it made me nervous. Could I not handle a boring life? Boring always sounded so nice when I was in the middle of things going sideways with a helping of everyone I love in mortal danger.

I heard footsteps on the stairs leading up to our apartment. Whoever it was wasn't being subtle. Nor had they set off the wards. Two sets of footsteps. Harper and Levi? Harper usually texted first these days.

"Ciaran and Brie," Alek said.

I let go of my magic but my apprehensive feelings grew. My neighbors wouldn't just pop over for a social call without warning. It wasn't exactly their old-school way. Unless something important that could only be discussed in person had come up.

Alek was in sweats but I only had a teeshirt on. Racing into our bedroom, I tugged on sweatpants. Alek went to open the door and I heard him greeting the leprechaun and the baker goddess as he invited them in.

Ciaran was dressed in one his red sweaters, as though the temperature of the evening outside wasn't still well over seventy. Brie's muscular frame was casually clad in a simple green teeshirt and pair of jeans. Their faces were solemn and neither returned my smile as I came into the kitchen.

"Not a social call?" I guessed, skipping the pleasantries since it seemed like they weren't in the mood.

"Sorry, Jade," Brie said. "I don't think this is good news."

"We've been called to Ireland, to the underbarrow." Ciaran spit the words out like they were sharp and might cut him. He flopped down into one of my kitchen chairs with a heavy sigh, running a hand through his copper and silver curls.

Brie remained standing.

I digested this news, remembering the last time they had been called away. The winter Samir attacked. From my friends' grim faces, they were recalling this, too.

"Did they give you a reason?" I said, leaning on the back of one of the chairs. "Do you want a cup of tea?" I added, remembering my manners.

"Ice tea?" Ciaran asked.

"Of course, with lots of sugar." I smiled and went to get him a glass.

"No explanation. No warning. I don't like it. Not while Iollan is away, either. But their demand was clear and we leave very early tomorrow morning." Brie nodded as I held up a second glass.

I distributed ice tea and finally Brie sat, her expression clouded as she sipped absently from the glass in her hand.

"There's been some whispers of trouble from the former Council of Nine," I said, glancing at Alek who had taken a chair beside me. I wasn't sure how much to say. I trusted Brie and Ciaran with my life, for they'd been there for all of us when it counted.

When they were able. They were Fey and answered to different laws and a different court than the rest of us.

"Storm is in the air," Brie said with a nod. "Don't know what form it'll take though. Just a feeling in my bones."

"All our bones, then," I said. I poked at the condensation on my glass but didn't drink. "Still, we'll manage. We always do."

"We'll send word if we can. Through Iollan." Ciaran drained his cup.

"Does he know?" I asked, thinking of poor Ezee, Iollan, and the honeymoon. The newlyweds would get no peace.

"We haven't told him. He'll be angry but there's nothing he can do and we didn't want to ruin his honeymoon." Brie pinned me with her gaze as she finished her tea.

"I won't breathe a word," I said. I wouldn't. I didn't want their special trip ruined either. "Not to Levi or anyone. Though your shops being closed will cause questions."

"We've taken care of that with notices on the doors. Family emergency," Ciaran said. His smile showed teeth but no mirth.

"Good luck, then," I said. "I'll try not to blow up anything in your absence." I meant it as a joke, but given past history, nobody laughed.

Brie and Ciaran left Alek and I sitting at the kitchen table, staring at four empty glasses. The invisible storm swirled somewhere out in the maybe horizon, danger coming for us sideways.

I found myself holding my talisman again, Samir's

gem digging a divot in my thumb as I pressed down. I wasn't good with threats I couldn't handle with a fireball or five. The trouble with the broken Council and whatever was about to happen that the Fey were planning for or dealing with was all nebulous still, danger potential but not realized. Sword of Damocles and all that shit.

"I'm gonna burn Samir's fucking door tomorrow," I said aloud.

"Let tomorrow be tomorrow," Alek said. He got to his feet and pulled me to mine. He didn't stop pulling until I was pressed against his warmth. "You promised me movie with war elephants." His breath was soft against my hair as he leaned down and kissed the top of my head.

I leaned into his chest and smiled, letting go of the talisman. Somehow, once again, Alek knew the right words.

5

Apparently our part of Idaho was in for one of the hottest summers on record and there was a high fire warning in effect. I was a good citizen and looked up burning regulations while I tried to form a plan for destroying the door without inadvertently destroying anything else.

So no legal door burning. I'd have to find a spot, like the old quarry, and set up a super safe circle to burn it in or something. It would have to wait.

"That was a big sigh," Harper commented from her chair by the counter in the game store.

Lara had the day off so she could get stuff done for finals, so it was just Harper and me holding down the fort. Not that there was much fort to be held down. Four people had stopped in already, but they were all locals asking if I knew why Brie's Bakery was closed even though she'd posted a sign. I just played dumb and repeated the story of family emergency even though the temptation to tell the truth and have nobody believe me was strong.

"County regulations blow," I said to Harper. "Can't just burn whatever you want when you want. And they say this is the land of freedom."

"What do you want to burn? Levi has a fire pit." Harper gave me a weird look over the top of her laptop screen.

"Samir sent me a door," I said. I figured the door thing would come out eventually anyway. Samir wasn't a topic I felt safe broaching with Harper though. There were still strained edges from what he'd done to her family. What he'd done to all of us.

"Like, an 'in case of my death mail this' sort of door?" Harper's green eyes narrowed.

"Basically. It's magic. I have no idea what it does, and I'm going to burn it to ashes as soon as I can." I folded my arms.

"Sweet. I'll help," she said with a smile best

described as gleefully homicidal.

The shop door chimed, saving me from having to awkwardly transition the conversation. Two middle-aged white men wearing dark suits entered. They looked serious, business-like even. My customers don't usually wear suits and try to look like TV FBI agents. I let magic sing in my veins as I warily walked a few steps toward them.

"Spycraft books are over there," I said, motioning toward the shelves full of RPGs.

"We're here to speak to you, Jade Crow," one of the men said. He was the older of the two and had a mustache that didn't quite fluff up to pornstache standards but could get there with time and care.

Now I was super on guard. Anyone who uses your full name like that is, in my experience, someone you never want to talk to.

"What about?" I said, putting some edge in my tone. Out of the corner of my eye I saw Harper put down her laptop and stand.

"Government business. Is there somewhere we can talk?" Stache said.

"Privately," the younger, blonder man added with a glance at Harper.

"Nah," I said. No way was I letting them get alone with me. Or me with them, given how much I was itching for a fight and it wasn't even their fault. "Here is good. Who are you and what do you want?"

"We're from the United States Government," Stache said. "We need to speak with you about Samir Cartwright."

Cartwright? I wondered how many names Samir had. He'd had so many lives. Taken so many lives. I pushed away the thought.

"What about him?" I said. "And do you have identification?" Because who introduces themselves as "from the Government" who is actually from the government? They hadn't set off the wards so they were probably human, but humans could be as dangerous as supernaturals. More so, in my experience, 'cause it was easy to underestimate them.

The men glanced at each other and then they both reached with deliberate slowness into their suits and produced flip folder ID cases straight out of television. I stepped closer, magic ready to shield or blast, and squinted at the IDs. Department of Homeland Security but with a small NoS designation under the official titles.

Not Otherwise Specified. I'd run into them before. I couldn't recall if they'd been under DHS or the FBI at that point. Clearly some reshuffling had happened since I'd broken my bio-dad out of one of their secret prisons.

They put away the IDs and I backed up a pace.

"We need to know where Samir is," Stache, whose ID had identified him as Special Agent Nichols, said.

"Good luck with that," I said. "I don't know shit, sorry. Samir and I are old news." I wondered if I should call a lawyer. But if they knew Samir was basically dead, why come ask me where he was?

"He came to Wylde, and hasn't been in contact with us since then," Agent Marksen, not Special, said.

"Sounds like a personal problem," Harper said. She came to my side, her hands on her hips. "He came, he killed some witches, he left." She was repeating the stuff that the NoS likely already knew, since their agent had been here when Peggy was murdered by Samir.

That same agent, Salazar, had helped me break out my bio-dad and I wasn't sure that was known. He had hopefully escaped but I had no idea what had happened after. It had been too chaotic at the time and my information line to people like that was severed since I'd had a falling out with the Archivist.

"Good luck, though," I said. "I'm sure if he wants to be in touch, he'll contact you. He's a dick that way." I made sure to use present tense.

Special Agent Nichols dropped the veneer of being friendly like it was an uncomfortable mask he was glad to shed. His eyes grew cold and his lips below his almost-impressive moustache turned pale as he pressed them against his teeth. I had to consciously not take a step back in the face of his naked hatred.

"Samir Cartwright was a Government asset. If you have knowledge of his whereabouts or are involved in his disappearance, you would be wise to volunteer that information, Jade Crow."

"Using people's full names is creepy," I said, keeping my tone mild. I let my magic out, wrapping tendrils of it around various small objects. My tea mug. A few plastic containers of dice I hadn't put prices on yet, the umbrella stand that nobody ever used but I kept by the door because it had dragons on it. With a mental tug I lifted every item into the air. Casually. Like you do.

"We don't know where Samir is. He's a murderous asshole and if he's crawled into a deep hole somewhere, good fucking riddance. If you want to talk to me after this, you can get in touch with my lawyer, Ms. Perkins at Perkins and Smitt." I made a mental note to call Perky as soon as these guys were out of my shop.

The agents backed up as Harper started to growl, their eyes darting around at the floating objects.

"This is unwise, Ms. Crow," Special Agent Nichols said. "Do not threaten us."

"Bye," I said, using more power to hold the door open.

Not special Agent Marksen caught his partner's arm as Nichols appeared to reach for his gun. A look passed between them. Special Agent Nichols chose to shoot me a glare instead of trying a bullet. Smartest thing he'd done since walking into my shop.

They left quickly, deliberately looking like they didn't give two fucks about the growling shifter or annoyed sorceress behind them. I let the objects down gently and reluctantly let go of my magic. Harper had followed the suits to the door.

"They got in to a dark sedan down the street, third guy driving," she said as she came back inside and closed the door behind herself. "How hard was it not to just rub yourself like this and be all 'he's in mah belleh'?"

I forced a grin even as my hand went to my talisman. Samir's heart gem felt like a proverbial stone in the shoe of my life. I hadn't found a good time to tell Harper that Samir was only mostly dead. I kept arguing with myself over if she really needed to know. I mean, he was pretty much as good as dead. But watching her do a silly little dance as she rubbed her stomach, I knew I had to say something. Secrets will eat a friendship alive if you let them fester.

"Hey, furball," I started to say, but then Blue October "She's My Ride Home" started playing from my phone. Alek's ringtone.

"What's up?" I figured something was up if he was calling instead of texting.

"Trouble," Alek said. "Can you come to Vivian's?"

"What kind of trouble?" I asked.

"I can watch the shop." Standing next to me, Harper could hear the phone call with her super shifter ears.

"Council trouble. Thank you, Harper," Alek said.

"On my way," I said. Alek hung up, not even saying goodbye. Tension made my teeth hurt and my skin prickle.

"Call me." Harper gave me a quick hug. "I got the shop sorted. Be safe."

"I'll let you know what it is when I know," I said, pushing away my frustration at Alek for not giving more details. But he didn't like to share things over the phone and it was probably smart anyway.

"Oh, shit, can you call Perky for me and warn her I might need a lawyer?" I added as I grabbed my keys.

"Consider it done. Just promise you won't go bust some heads without me if that's what has to get done."

"Promise, furball," I said. My mind was already racing across town to the vet and secret shifter doctor Vivian's office and home. If she was involved, someone was probably hurt.

I hated that my next thought was that if someone was hurt, someone was responsible. And if someone was responsible, there was someone to fight. Finally.

Vivian's clinic was in a large house on the other side of town from my store. She had a closed sign up on the window which was unusual for this time of day but spoke to how serious the situation inside must be. Alek opened the door even before I'd made it onto the porch.

"Better you come in," he said, seeing my questioning expression.

I squeezed his hand and followed him through the reception area into the back, all the way back to Vivian's large personal office. Alek had once almost died on the floor there and I repressed a shiver as we entered the crowded room. I'd watched him almost die too many times.

Vivian was hovering near a dark-haired Asian woman who was stretched out on a cot, propped up with paper-covered pillows. The woman was the only person I didn't know in the room. She looked somewhere in her thirties but given shifter aging, I knew she was likely much older. Her eyes were striking, light brown on the inside of the irises merging to dark grey rings. She squeezed them shut as Vivian did something hidden from me by the vet's body.

Levi and Junebug had positioned themselves against the back wall by the rear door. Levi gave me a half-wave and Junebug a strained smile as I nodded to them in greeting. The rest of the space was taken up by Carlos, Alek's Justice mentor and friend. The huge black lion-shifter stood up from where he was leaning against a desk that looked like it might give up under his weight.

"Fix her," Carlos all but growled at me.

"Carlos," the woman on the cot said as she opened her eyes. Her tone was admonishing but gentle, the way one might speak to someone they knew well. Or loved. "I am May Cheung," she said, her gaze moving to meet mine.

"May was a prime Justice to the Council of Nine," Alek said.

"Hi," I said, looking back at the woman. Her smile was pained. Vivian moved and I saw the thick white bandaging around May's chest and belly. "I don't know what a prime Justice is," I added, glancing up at Alek. "And I'm not a healer."

It was May who answered me. "Justices assigned to directly assist Council members. And to train to take their place, to take on the mantle once the burden grew too great."

"Okay, back up even further here. What mantle?" I blinked at her. Alek had always been tight-lipped about the Council of Nine and I hadn't pressed too much. I knew they had some kind of foresight or visions that they imparted to their Justices to stop crimes, but it seemed like there was more to it.

"Is there time for this?" Carlos asked. "You are hurt, we need…"

"The Council could stop crimes, could send us to punish the guilty, because they were given the gift of seeing the future, or at least possible futures, by the Fates," May spoke over Carlos, her voice low but strong. "Seeing the future is a difficult thing. It can drive you mad. It did drive the First mad. That is why we are here."

"Don't move," Vivian said as May struggled to sit up more. "You'll start bleeding again."

"The First, the one who sent those wolves to threaten the Alpha of Alphas? Is he the one who tried to kill you and Alek in New Orleans?" I leaned into Alek, trying to put the pieces together.

Carlos nodded. His expression was tight with worry but his lips pressed together in resignation as he accepted that explanations were coming before action. I didn't know how to explain that I couldn't take action when I didn't know what was going on. And I wasn't some cleric who magically handed out health potions. I didn't even know what May's wound looked like under all that bandaging.

"The First has killed all the other Council Members. Mine was unable to pass the mantle to me before he got her. He did this to me," May added, wincing as she moved her arm to gesture to the bandaging. "Wounds that won't heal."

I wrapped my arms around myself as a shiver worked its way down my spine. Wolf, my spirit guardian, had given Samir a wound that didn't heal. It was the only time I'd heard of anything like that happening.

"Who is the First?" I said, then I shook my head. "No, *what* is the First?"

There was no way we were dealing with a normal shifter, not if a room full of capable, powerful shifters looked this freaked out. Levi was uncharacteristically silent, just standing against the wall with his arm over Junebug's shoulders. I wondered why they were here, how they were connected to this, but it didn't feel like the right time to ask.

May, Alek, and Carlos all exchanged looks that likely meant more than I could read into them. It was Alek who spoke.

"As far as anyone knows, he is the oldest shifter alive. He has powers, magical abilities, that no other shifter has ever had. It was he who would grant or take away Justice powers."

"I assume he's revoked all of your powers?" I asked, looking at the three Justices in turn.

Carlos and May nodded. I looked up at Alek again.

"Not mine," he said softly.

"He wants Alek for some reason," May said. "Before he killed…" she trailed off and took a couple shallow breaths. "He was clear that he has a plan for Alek. Alek was proposed as his successor, years ago."

So we had a murderous super powerful shifter with the ability to see the future and undefined magical abilities who apparently wanted everyone in this room dead except for my lover who he had a special probably awful plan for. Oh, and if the warning given to Freyda was any indication, he was also forming an army of shifters.

Sounded like a job for Jade Crow, murderer of evil peeps who want to kill awesome peeps she loves as well as other peeps who are probably also cool.

I was going to have to work on a better super hero job title.

"So he can give you guys extra powers like making shifters, uh, shift. And he can see the future. Anything else I should know before I go kick his ass?" I tried on a smile. It was more pressing my lips to my teeth but I went with it.

"She's serious?" May said to Alek.

"Most of the time." His arm was strong and warm as he wrapped it around my shoulders.

"He can take over minds," Carlos said. The grim tone of his words took what little levity was left in the room. "He has to be close enough for you to hear his voice, but once he has control, it is almost impossible to break without putting a great distance between him and the affected."

"Just shifter minds?" I asked. I had enough voices in my head, I didn't want to fight someone who would add another.

"Most likely?" May said. "I've never seen him do it to anyone else. And not all shifters are susceptible. He was unable to do it to the other Council members, for example."

"So there's a future-seeing, mind-controlling powerful shifter dude with maybe other magical powers raising a shifter army and coming for my boyfriend? Is that all?" I'd wanted a fight but should have remembered that whole careful what you wish for phrase. The Universe is a bitch sometimes.

"That's the gist," Carlos said. "We should not stay in Wylde. They'll be hunting us."

"Can you look at these wounds?" Vivian asked me.

"I'm not a healer," I said again. But I couldn't resist their desperate eyes so I moved out from under Alek's arm and toward May. "I'm way better at killing people than making them whole again."

"I'm dying," May said. "I cannot shift. It won't let me, the pain knocks me out if I even consider it. You can hardly make it worse."

Oh, ye of little faith, I thought but held my tongue as I knelt beside her. I summoned magic and held my hands over the bandages. I couldn't see what the wounds looked like, but I decided to start with a simple kind of detect magic spell.

I wasn't expecting to find much. Shifter powers are very different from sorcery or even human magics. Magic doesn't affect them as well and sorcerers can't eat their hearts and gain anything but a stomachache. But wounds that don't heal sounded magical to me and it was the only thing I could think to start with.

Power, raw twisting raging red power slammed into my seeking magic and physically knocked me onto my ass as I threw up a shield. The magic to my internal senses was like a pissed off lava snake, coiled and burning everything it touched.

The smell of the foreign magic was sulfurous, hot, tinged with the acrid bite of burning hair. It was different from my magic, but in the way that Samir's was different. Or Tess. But it told me something we hadn't known before. This spell revealed the First to me. Only... it was not possible.

"Sorcery," I said. "This is sorcery. Like from a sorcerer."

"The First has many abilities," May said with a gasp as the snake reacted to my prodding.

"He's a sorcerer," I said aloud. "How the fuck is that possible?"

"A shifter and a sorcerer?" Levi spoke up. "Are you sure?"

"I'm staring at sorcery right now," I said through gritted teeth as I examined the burning snake thing. May was right, she was dying. This spell had to be removed.

"You are a sorceress born to shifters," Alek said. "Perhaps the First is the same, somehow."

"What's his shifter form?" I asked. I was technically a shifter, if you counted being able to turn into a dragon as shifting. Except I couldn't shift into a dragon on this plane cause of some magical seals keeping the world from being overrun by magical critters.

"He has three," May said. "Snake, eagle, tiger."

"Chimaera," Levi said with a low whistle. "I thought they were myth."

"So did I," Carlos said, eyes narrowing. Apparently May hadn't told him everything.

But hey, not a dragon. So that was a plus. I kept the relief to myself since only a few people in this room knew I was a dragon.

"So he's a shifter and a sorcerer," I said. "We'll deal with it." I sounded a lot more sure than I felt. But what choice did we have? I wasn't going to let him take Alek or hurt anyone else if I could help it.

"Can you fix me?" May asked, her brown-grey eyes reflecting dim hope.

"I might kill you trying," I said, sensing this was a woman who appreciated honesty.

"Do it," she said.

"May," Carlos started to say but May shook her head even though it was clear the gesture pained her.

"Get out, all of you," she said. "Just Jade."

I didn't argue. I had no idea what the spell snake thing would do once I started really poking it. Alek squeezed my shoulder and led everyone out of the room. Carlos went last. He shot me a look that was half warning, half desperation. I gave him what I hoped was a competent, assured nod.

After the door closed behind them, I caught May's gaze and held it.

"Seriously, this might kill you."

She nodded, closed her eyes, and slowly let out her breath. Her entire body relaxed into the cot.

"Begin," she murmured.

I concentrated on the lava snake. The magic was coiled around her torso like a constrictor. Magic doesn't last forever unless it is fixed to a source or an object. I wasn't good with magical objects, that was Samir's strength. But I knew enough to know that this spell had to be anchored somehow. I followed the coils of the snake, using my own magic to shield me from the burning, sulfurous tendrils of power that tried to latch onto me.

There. The tail of the snake was attached to a glowing orange-red ember. A physical thing.

"What did he attack you with?" I asked, fighting to maintain concentration and magical sight on the ember.

"A sword with many whip-like blades. Urumi, it's called." May's voice sounded as though she was speaking through thick cloth.

Urumi. So the First had an exotic weapon proficiency. I wished Levi or Harper were there so I could make the joke aloud. I filed it away for telling them later.

"Was it unusual in any way?" I asked instead. "Pieces on the ends?"

"It glittered," she said. "I remember that."

My best guess was that the urumi was bespelled so that any wounds created would end up with particles of ensorcelled metal, spawning the lava snake currently killing the Justice. Death by glitter.

"Okay, this is going to suck," I muttered.

May didn't answer but she was still breathing so I figured she was ready as she was going to get.

I shaped my magic with my will, pushing it into tongs. I pictured them like dry ice, pure cold, a cold so freezing it would burn. The coils reacted before I even touched them, drawing back, away from the chill of my magic. May screamed.

I thrust the tongs into the heart of the lava snake, reaching for the ember there. For a glorious moment I had it clutched in my power, turning dark and cold from the bitter bite of my icy spell.

Then it slipped free, worming its way deeper as though alive, propelled by the First's sorcery.

"Fuck." I pushed after it but the heat grew, overwhelming my power. I fed more and more into my ice tongs, forming them sharper as I dug into the lava trying to destroy my spell.

There. The ember, burning brighter, glowing almost white. I smashed icy magic into it, wrapping it up like an unwanted gift before yanking it toward me, free of the coils.

May screamed a final time and went silent.

The burning coils turned to ash and the sudden lack of heat made me shiver as I reeled back onto my heels. A tiny piece of silver metal rested in my hand.

There was blood everywhere and May wasn't moving. Shit.

"May," I said, reaching to shake her. Her bloody bandages squished beneath my hand, almost too hot to touch. "You have to shift."

"I am tired, my love," she whispered in Spanish.

"You must change shape," I replied in the same language, using the formal imperative. I softened it by saying, "Please. Live."

Her brown-grey eyes flew open. Then she was no longer a blood-covered woman but a silver and black snow leopard. She twisted to her side and then flopped as though that was the maximum effort she could give. Her eyes were bluer in this form but still with a ring of brown at the iris. She blinked slowly at me before closing them with a long sigh.

I walked out of the room in an exhausted daze. Fighting the First's spell had required two things I'm not good at—precision, and ice. I'm much more a fireball kind of girl. But I'd saved her. Maybe. I stared down at the metal in my bloody hand.

I'd wanted a fight, a name to put on this impending storm.

"Is she?" Carlos asked me as I walked into the tense air of the reception area. He looked ready to pounce, his eyes narrowing as he saw the blood on me.

"She's shifted, and is alive," I said, holding up the bit of metal. "I think I got what was killing her."

Carlos pushed past me. Vivian nodded at me with a small smile and followed Carlos to the office to check on May.

"Why are you here?" I asked Levi. "Wait, that sounded harsh, sorry."

"Nah," Levi said. He tugged on a lip piercing and looked at Junebug.

"I'm pregnant," Junebug said.

When humans say that, I always wondered if I should offer congrats. With shifters, given how hard it is for them to conceive, I never had to wonder.

"Shit, congrats!" I found I could still smile after all.

"We were going to wait and tell everyone once Ezee got back, cause he'll kill me for not telling him first," Levi said.

"My lips are sealed." I closed my fist. The little scrap of silvery metal dug into my palm.

Alek came up behind me and pulled me against his chest. I let myself sag into him with my eyes closed. I'd move and wash off May's blood in a minute. For now it felt good to be held.

"How fucked are we?" Levi said after a long, awkward moment.

I opened my eyes again and made a face. "Maybe you should get out of town for a while," I said, knowing it was pointless. Knowing even with a baby on the way, neither of them were going to do the smart thing and go.

"We're going to pretend you didn't say that," Junebug said. If she'd been in her owl form her feathers would have ruffled right up.

My clean hand found my talisman and Samir's heart.

"We'll fight," I said.

"Together," Levi said.

"Always." I looked up at Alek and he pressed his lips to my forehead.

Which is how Sheriff Lee found us when she walked into the clinic wearing an expression that said our already exhausting day was about to get worse.

7

Stonebrook Hunting Lodge was its official, human world name, but everyone just called it The Den. The Den was the seat of Freyda, the Alpha of Alphas, the top wolf-shifter in the western Hemisphere, and someone I had come to consider a friend. Alek drove us up the long, winding road through pristine old-growth forest as I sat with a growing knot in my stomach.

The Den was a faux-castle, a huge wood and stone structure complete with towers and a three-story Great Hall. The stones glinted in the sunlight and the whole place felt eerily still as we drove into the large parking lot. The lot was more than half full, which was unusual. The bulk of Freyda's pack lived here and around in houses hidden back in the forest, though some lived in town as well, but I'd rarely seen this many cars here, especially after Freyda had decided to close the lodge to guests after her father passed.

Rachel, aka Sheriff Lee, followed us up in her SUV. She'd only told us that Freyda needed me to come look at something, and that the wolf had stressed how urgent it was that Rachel find me. When pressed she'd said that her impression was someone was hurt and it might be magical sort of damage since they wanted a sorceress present. Which was not at all comforting given what I'd just dealt with in Vivian's office.

It seemed the First was going to make damn sure my life wasn't boring from here on out. I couldn't wait to track the bastard down and show him how tired of assholes and their stupid evil games I was.

Rachel led us up to one of the small doors flanking the Great Hall. Just a couple years ago, though it felt like a lifetime now, I'd come in this door and stopped a bomb from going off and killing every Alpha in the Western hemisphere. I took a deep breath before I went inside, steadying myself. Alek gave my hand a squeeze before letting it go and all but crowding me through the door and into the huge room beyond.

There were half a dozen people in the hall, two of them were shifted into giant wolves. One wolf was reddish in color with a shaggy mane of deeper red, the other pure white. The two people who had been sitting on one of the benches arrayed against the far wall half rose at our entrance but Freyda, standing with a dark-haired man near the wolves, waved them down with a quick, casual gesture. The shifters sat back down with worried, tense expressions, but they nodded at Alek and Rachel. I didn't recognize either the man or the woman, but their faces were familiar and I figured they must be part of Freyda's pack.

The man with Freyda turned and I found myself smiling even though his face was grim. Aurelio, called Softpaw by his pack, hadn't changed much since I'd last seen him. His beard was shorter, hardly more than a long shadow on his brown face. He still had the streak of white in his black hair and golden-brown eyes that were far older than the face they rested in. He was wearing a pair of grey sweatpants and a dark green teeshirt, which was twice as much clothing as I usually saw him in. I swallowed a comment about it being a special occasion as I took in the tension in his and Freyda's shoulders.

"Jade," Aurelio said. "Thank you for coming."

"I could hardly ignore a summons," I said, smiling at Freyda to take any bite from my words. She returned my smile without teeth and inclined her head.

"Bird, Snowdrop, move," Aurelio said, looking at the two wolves.

They slunk aside, revealing a man unconscious on a makeshift pallet of blankets. He was maybe an inch or two taller than I and his sandy hair was plastered to his pale brow with sweat. As I watched he shifted as though dreaming, his body restless. His face was vaguely familiar, though I couldn't place where I'd seen him. From Aurelio's wolves posture, I guessed he was part of their pack.

I didn't have to reach for magic to feel the spell on him. Pulled by the cotton-candy scent of foreign magic, I cautiously approached. The two wolves had drawn away only far enough for me to reach the unconscious man and they sank down onto their haunches, watching me intently.

"Can you back off a little more?" I asked the white wolf, trying not to sound nervous. They were shifters, but they were Aurelio's pack, and his pack always seemed less human than other shifters, more wild.

They lived in the woods and ate raw meat, after all. Not my cup of tea. Probably they had no tea ever.

The two wolves glanced back at Aurelio and must have gotten some signal for they both retreated another half dozen feet. Good enough.

"Who is he?" I asked. "And what happened to him?" I summoned my own magic and sent a testing tendril out, my hand hovering over the restless shifter. The nagging sense of familiarity with his face grew. "Do I know him?"

The cotton-candy magic seemed to wrap the man like swaddling clothes but it didn't react to my magic. A passive effect of some kind? I wasn't sure. Whatever spell he was under, it was done by another magic user. I couldn't tell yet if it was sorcery or human magic. However, the smell was wrong for it to be the First, which was a relief even if it only brought on more questions.

"You met Johnny briefly during the trouble before, after my father died," Freyda said. "He was part of my pack. His mate was killed last fall in that horrible truck crash."

"That drunk driver?" I asked, recalling the accident. Freyda nodded. Three people had died, including the driver. It was a tragedy for any town, but especially one as small as Wylde. I suppressed a shiver. I had nearly killed Alek and I last summer when I hit a moose and it had taken a while before I'd wanted to get behind the wheel. I could only imagine the grief Johnny must have felt, the helplessness. The anger.

"He's called Halfheart, now," Aurelio said. He crouched by my side but didn't touch the man. "He disappeared a few days ago and we tracked him to a human camp. I was worried he'd attack the humans, he'd come to us so angry at humans. But they'd captured him. Had him chained up."

"What happened to the humans?" Alek asked and I suppressed a totally inappropriate grin. He might not be a Justice anymore, but old habits died hard for my mate.

"They were extremely well-armed," Aurelio said, frustration in his voice. "We stayed out of sight and waited to see if we could get him free. But they released him the next morning, at dawn. Only, he wasn't the same."

The red wolf snarled and the white wolf gave a soft whine. Freyda and Aurelio both growled at them and they fell silent.

"She's going to help," Aurelio said.

I rubbed at the gooseflesh on my forearms and resisted the urge to throw up a magic shield. I wasn't at my limit yet, but fighting the lava snake inside May hadn't exactly been a walk in the proverbial park. I had a feeling I was going to be using more magic before too long.

"He's been broken," Freyda said, her eyes flicking from me to Alek and back. "He's been severed. Softpaw had to knock him unconscious and keep him that way just to get him here."

"Severed?" I asked, hoping they didn't mean what I thought they might mean.

"Are you sure?" Alek said at the same time, his own voice a growl.

"I am sure," Aurelio said. He licked his lips and squared his shoulders as though a decision had been made. "I have telepathy," he added. "I can link to minds, if they allow it. Halfheart has been cut off from his wolf. He cannot shift. He cannot reach into the shadow wood and become his other half."

"How is that possible?" I asked even as I turned my gaze and my magic back to the unconscious man. Sorcery. That was how. I had a feeling that whatever this was, it was definitely a sorcerer. Magic like that, I'd never heard of it being possible. From the expression on my shifter companion's faces, it wasn't a common thing, more like some horrible story shifters whispered over camp fires to give each other nightmares.

"It is something the Council could do," Alek said. "But they stopped after the first few, deciding death was better. Severing a shifter is a fate worse than death."

"This isn't the First's magic," I said. "It's the wrong smell."

Aurelio, Freyda, and Alek all nodded as though that made perfect sense. Which, given how they probably interpreted the world with their preternatural senses, it likely did.

"But it is sorcery?" Aurelio said.

"I think so. It could be a different kind of magic, but if it is, we're still dealing with a very powerful or competent magic-user."

"Can you fix it?"

I looked into his hopeful golden-brown eyes and sighed. "I don't know. Undoing a spell isn't like pulling apart a sweater. It can be more like uncooking a meal. Or unburning a piece of paper. Some things don't go back."

I hated to extinguish the hope in his eyes, and I hated the way the heads of the two wolves flanking us drooped, their ears flattening. I wished I could wave a magic wand and promise the world to the people around me who clearly cared for the broken man lying in front of us.

"One more thing," Aurelio said, his gaze still intently on my face. "He said your name, right before I put him out."

That didn't totally creep me out at all. Not a bit. I suppressed another shiver even though the hall was far from cold. It probably meant nothing. Johnny aka Halfheart had known of me and might have realized that if sorcery had fucked him over, sorcery could maybe save him. It wasn't totally illogical.

"I'll see what I can do for him," I said. "Might want to back away. Magic can do weird shit when poked, especially if this is sorcery."

If it wasn't sorcery, it would have more pattern to it, and there was always a chance I could undo it. If it was sorcery, my best chance to fix it would be to find the sorcerer and eat his or her heart. Which was a thought I shoved deep into a reinforced chest in my head and slammed the lid on. I knew in my head I'd have to kill the First that way, unless I used the Alpha and Omega magical dagger the way I had with Samir, but I was not thinking about that issue. I was not thinking about it really fucking hard. Nope.

Not thinking about Samir at all, promise, I clutched my D20 talisman with my left hand and put my right hand on Halfheart, formerly Johnny's, chest. The cotton-candy scented cocoon of magic did not react as I slid my own magic down into his body, looking for some kind of root or basis for the spell.

There was nothing at first, not even a kernel. It felt like the magic I felt and smelled was residual, a byproduct of what had been done. His heartbeat was irregular beneath my palm, his bare chest slick with sweat. He thrashed his head back and forth and I heard Aurelio suck in a breath behind me.

"He's waking."

"Let him," I told Aurelio, not wanting whatever telepathic power the Bitterroot Alpha had to interfere with my own magic.

I let go of my talisman and crawled forward so I was straddling Halfheart. I pinned his arms with my hands, knowing I wasn't strong enough to stop a shifter from moving me out of the way like a sack of flour if he wanted. I poured magic into my hands and along his arms, over his chest, using it to hold him down, keep him still.

"Johnny," I said as his startlingly blue eyes opened and blinked at me. "Halfheart. It's okay. Do you remember me? I'm Jade, and I'm going to help you." Or try. But I left that bit off.

"Jade," he said, his voice sounding like it had to travel a hundred miles uphill over loose gravel to escape his throat. The cotton-candy scent grew stronger and I wrapped a shield around the two of us on instinct.

"Yes," I said. "That's right. I'm here to help. Just relax."

The magic was reacting now, building from somewhere inside him and rising from his skin like steam. I tried to follow it back into him, now that he was awake and the spell, whatever it was, had come alive. I had a slim hope that perhaps he wasn't really severed. That instead this magic was keeping him from shifting, from even sensing his wolf half, much like the magic I'd fought earlier had kept May from changing shape. I had the unnerving thought that apparently sorcery could affect shifters far more than I'd ever been given to understand, and that my friends might be more vulnerable than I wanted to contemplate, but the fleeting worry was burned away by the rising tide of power. It wasn't a cocoon anymore but a cloud.

"Jade Crow," Halfheart said in that rough, far away voice. "Good."

I had no warning. Just a sense of incredible emptiness inside of Halfheart, as the magic seemed to give way and I saw into him. It was like watching a spider thread drifting on the wind over a barren plain. Vastness and hollowness and loss like I could hardly comprehend, the feeling of all the grief in the world slamming into a space so large nothing could ever fill it.

Then Halfheart exploded.

Levi would also joke when we'd watch anime that while the IRL human body might have about eight pints of blood, in the animated universe clearly it was more like eighty and highly pressurized to boot. I'd laughed about it at the time.

I wasn't laughing anymore. Levi had never had the singular experience of a body exploding all over him.

My eyes wouldn't open and for a moment I couldn't get my arms to respond either. The explosion had slammed me back into the shield I'd thrown up around Johnny and me, knocking the wind out of me from both directions as I pancaked, caught between bursting body and magic shield.

"Jade?" Alek's voice was muffled, as though my ears needed to pop.

Which from the pressure in and on my head, they probably did. I opened my mouth, half in an effort to respond and half to see if I could relieve the pressure. Mistake of epic, bloody proportions. Gore and blood coated my mouth and face and a chunk of something I didn't want to think about too hard fell into my open mouth.

I spit it out as Alek helped me sit up. A piece of cloth wiped over my face and I realized my eyes had been glued shut with human parts debris. I blinked, sucking in another breath as my ears finally popped.

Blood was everywhere around me. Soaking me, the floor around me, the blankets Johnny had been lying on. Stinging in the cuts along my arms and legs. There was nothing left of him. Even his bones had pulverized, which explained the rips and tears in my clothing and the myriad of small wounds I was starting to feel all too clearly.

Eighty *gallons* of pressurized blood, more like. I was glad Levi wasn't there, for a lot of reasons.

"Shh, just breathe," Alek murmured as I blinked at him.

With my ears working better now I could hear Freyda telling someone to get more towels. Towels sounded nice. I blinked again, exhaustion and pain doing battle to see which could keep me awake and which could push me under. I wanted to curl into a hot bath and sleep for a thousand years without dreams of a terrified man's blue eyes staring at me as the world exploded into cotton-candy flavored blood and gore. Looking down at my shredded jeans, I winced. That was almost definitely a piece of intestine resting on my thigh.

Alek followed my gaze and brushed the grey-brown slippery-looking chunk off me. Aurelio handed him a huge towel and Alek bundled me up despite my muttered protest. I was glad for the detergent-scented black towel that hid the sight of myself from me but gladder for the strength of Alek's arms as he lifted me away from the circle of gore.

"We have to stop meeting like this," I said to Freyda, repressing what might have looked like a crazy-person kind of smile. I wasn't thinking clearly and I knew it.

"Why did he…" she trailed off as she made a wide gesture with her arms.

"I don't know," I said, only partially lying. I had felt the spell, laid like a trap inside him, waiting for the right trigger. I wasn't certain, not fully, but it was like it had been waiting for me. My mind was spinning down the drain of exhaustion and I couldn't hold on to the speculating thoughts whirling around it. I needed rest.

"She needs to rest and heal," Alek said, forestalling any other questions. "I am taking her home." He looked at Aurelio. "Come tomorrow morning? I am sure she will have questions for you."

"And I for her," Aurelio said as he exchanged a heavy glance with Freyda.

"I'm right here," I muttered but my protest was as weak as I felt. I needed rest. I needed time to think. Two sorcerers possibly gunning for the Wylde shifter population was two too many.

Though I had a feeling, recalling that far away, gritty voice, that sorcerer number two was after me, instead. I wormed one hand through the wet mess of my teeshirt and felt for my D20. It was still there, Samir's heart a strangely comforting bump against my thumb. I felt like Gandalf asking Frodo if the ring was safe.

"Shower," I said to Alek. "Please."

"Here, take her to my quarters," Freyda said. "It's closer than your home."

That sounded like a solid plan to me since it was a quicker path to hot water and hopefully less blood. I nodded at Alek's unasked question and he changed direction, following Freyda from the hall.

Closing my eyes, I rubbed Samir's heart gem. I had thought him an evil dick, which he was, truly, but part of me, a tiny traitorous part, could see the merit in just offing every other sorcerer. They were sure a fucking destructive lot in my short experience with most of the ones who had crossed my path. Shoving that thought away, I leaned into Alek's warmth and dreamed of soap.

I vaguely recalled Alek getting me into the shower. The sting of water in the fresh cuts on my skin. The relief I felt as the pain faded and the blood washed away. I wanted my own bed and I think I said something aloud about it but sleep was calling my name as loud as I'd ever heard it.

I remembered Wolf leaning into me, visible only to myself and acting very oddly. I remembered a thread of panic hanging like a lifeline thrown by my brain to what little conscious thought I was still capable of.

I remembered thinking I shouldn't be this tired. That I must be hurt worse than I thought.

And I remembered the smell of spun sugar. Pink wisps of sugar. Spinning and spinning and wrapping around me until everything else was unimportant and I sank into a sugar cloud and slept.

I awoke alone in a strange room. The walls were bare grey stone, so I figured I was still at the Den. They must have decided not to take me home after all. The bed was narrow and the room hardly larger than my almost palatial new bathroom in my apartment. It was also empty of anyone but myself, which I found odd and alarming. Something must have happened.

"Alek?" I called out. My voice reverberated from the stone walls.

There was no window, just a single door. I pushed off the heavy black quilt and put my bare feet on the stone floor. The stone was surprisingly warm and smooth against my toes. I was wearing only a long black teeshirt that said "Death Before Decaf" across the chest, one of my favorites to sleep in. Alek must have had someone bring it from home, I thought. There was no way he'd have left my side.

Except he wasn't at my side. My sense of wrongness growing I reached for my talisman.

That's when I truly panicked. It wasn't there. Nothing was around my neck.

Alek wouldn't have removed it. I pushed down the panic and ran for the door, throwing it wide. Nobody would touch the D20. Nobody. They knew better.

"Alek?" I called out again as I burst into an empty corridor. Stone walls lined a narrow hall in both directions. No other doors visible.

"Jade?"

I didn't recognize the voice but it could have been Alek's. It was male, but muffled and echoing at the same time, as though it came from far away.

"Alek? Where are you?" Where is my damn talisman, I wanted to scream but I held it in.

Growling echoed down the seemingly endless corridor as I picked a direction and went in it, my dread growing. I reached for magic and hit a wall inside myself.

No, not a wall. A cocoon. As though my power were

wrapped in layer after layer of gauze. Had I exhausted myself that much fighting the First's lava creature and then containing the mystery explosion spell? I hadn't thought so.

Again I reached for a talisman that wasn't there. The growling grew and I heard my name again. Definitely Alek's voice this time.

Picking up my pace, I ran down the hallway. I had to find him. Something was horribly wrong and I couldn't get to my magic. I ripped at the gauze inside me with mental fingers, hunting for the feel of my power. My feet slapped on the stone, echoing and downing out the sound of Alek's voice as he called my name.

"Jade!"

I skidded to a stop as the corridor turned abruptly. Aurelio stood in front of me. His hair was a tangled mess, his eyes golden-brown sparks in the dim light.

"Where is everyone?" I asked. "What's happened?"

"Jade," Aurelio said again, reaching a hand toward me. "I'll take you to them. But we have to make sure the heart is safe first."

I almost reached for the missing talisman again but stopped mid-gesture.

Aurelio didn't know about Samir's heart. If he thought anything about it he would be in the camp that thought I'd killed my evil ex.

"What heart?" I asked. I took a deep slow breath and stopped trying to unwrap my magic.

"Samir's heart," Aurelio said. "We have to make sure it is safe. Where did you hide it?"

I didn't have a magical spinning top or the like, but relief flooded through me and I laughed.

"I'm dreaming," I said aloud. "Oh thank the fucking universe."

Aurelio's face shifted slightly, growing uglier, his mouth twisting into a snarl.

"This isn't a game, Jade," he said, his voice sounding less and less like the Softpaw I knew. "We have to make sure it is safe, it's important. Life and death."

"Who are you?" I asked. The growling was louder and I felt Wolf's presence nearby. She was breaking into the dream, freeing me from the magic holding me here.

"Where is the heart?" Not-Aurelio snarled.

Cotton-candy scent turned to burning sugar around me as Wolf, huge and dark and beautifully deadly, slammed into him. Her teeth ripped into Not-Aurelio's neck before I could ask anything else.

"Jade!" Alek's voice again. Louder. Pain, gloriously real, dug into my shoulders and neck.

Wolf, her starry-night eyes glowing, howled as she dropped the torn, unbleeding body. And the walls came down around us.

I woke up in my own bed to Alek's relieved face. His hands dug into my shoulders where he was holding me upright. I knew I'd have bruises for a day or so from the pressure of his grip but I didn't care. The room was dim though I could see sunlight poking through the edges of the blinds, but my view was taken up mostly by an extremely concerned Alek. I leaned into him and kissed his chin.

"I'm okay," I murmured. His scent was deliciously cotton-candy-free and its usual heady mix of musk and spice. He was real. I was free.

The dream, or spell dream, or whatever the fuck that had been, swamped my thoughts as the tide of relief I felt at being awake and free faded back. Alek released me and I reached for my D20. Samir's heart gem was still in its spot but I needed more reassurance.

"Alpha and Omega," I said, looking at the nightstand where the dagger usually rested. It was still there, solid and waiting. I summoned my magic, letting power fill my veins and push the nightmare farther away. I stopped short of using magic to levitate the blade to me and leaned toward it instead, my aching body protesting the stretch.

"Jade," Alek started to say, a warning tone in his voice that I ignored in my rush to make sure Samir's heart was as dead as it could be. He caught my reaching arm with his hand.

"Mystery sorcerer knows about Samir's heart," I said, forestalling him as I wiggled more upright. "Give me the damn knife. I have to make sure it stays dormant. Just fucking humor me, okay? I'll explain in a second."

Alek grimaced and shook his head slowly as he released my arm.

"Samir's... heart? The heart you ate and destroyed? That heart?" Harper's voice came from behind my mate. "I think you'll explain now."

Fuck. Fuck toast on a fuck stick.

I'd just faced a lava snake, an exploding person booby-trap, and a spell-induced interrogation nightmare. But all that had been a lazy stroll in the proverbial park compared to the blender of anger, grief, and betrayal in Harper's voice.

"Harper," I said. "Just give me a moment. Please."

Alek rose and picked up the Alpha and Omega from the nightstand, holding it out to me. I sagged into the pillows, flinching away from the look in Harper's green eyes as she approached the foot of the bed.

"I'll be outside," Vivian, who I also hadn't noticed, said from the doorway of the bedroom.

None of us responded to her and she slunk away. I wished I could follow.

"Furball," I said softly but she shook her head violently.

"Don't you fucking furball me, and stop. Lying." Harper spit out the words.

I pulled the dagger free of its sheath. The Alpha and Omega is technically two blades but they could merge into one. Sometimes they turned into a sword. The magic in them was incredibly old and outside anything in my experience, but supposedly they could destroy anything. The knife was how I had killed Samir without having to kill him.

"The magic in this blade keeps his heart, his entire self, reduced to this tiny gem," I said to Harper as I touched the tip of the blade to the ruby-looking gem fixed into the one spot on my D20 talisman. "He's dead, for all intents and purposes. I just didn't eat his heart." The gem flared with red light and then went dull again as the knife touched it.

Samir's heart was secret and it was safe, but it certainly wasn't my precious. I wished I could throw it into a fucking volcano right that damn second if it would take the look of pain and betrayal off my best friend's face.

I thought of the nightmare interrogation. Not so secret, perhaps. Maybe not safe, either.

"So you didn't kill him. He's right there," Harper said, making a curt gesture toward my talisman.

"He's just a tiny drop of rock-like blood. He's basically dead," I said. I knew I had been wrong not to tell her, but it hadn't seemed quite so stupid at the time. There had been logic and love and sparing of feelings or something, but looking at her face all my justifications and excuses felt like tissue paper against the bonfire of her anger.

"You lied to me," Harper snarled. She looked like she might spring at me and Alek stepped toward her.

"Azalea," he murmured in a warning tone, using Harper's real name. Which was probably a mistake since she hated that name.

"Fuck off," she snarled at him, too. "My own best friend Obi-Wan Kenobi'd on me. I think being fucking angry is pretty okay right now."

"Whoa," I said, putting the Alpha and Omega down. I folded a bit of the comforter over the knife, not wanting the super dangerous weapon in view at the moment. "That's a little harsh. Samir is harmless, dead for all intents and purposes. I'm sorry I let you believe I'd eaten him. But I couldn't. I can't end the world, Harper. I can't."

"How do you know?" she said. "How do you really know if killing him would end it or not? And how do you fucking know that what you are doing with that magic blade is really keeping him 'mostly dead'? Cause from where I'm standing, this looks like a recipe for a big old super villain come back if I've ever seen one. Obi-Wan."

I tucked the D20 into my shirt. I hadn't exactly

dropped Samir in a volcano and walked away but though it hurt to admit, I guess I was kind of leaving a door open for my nemesis to return, ala Kenobi.

"Okay, fair enough. But I can't take the chance that Brie and my father are right, that truly killing him would cause a magic apocalypse. Please, you have to see how I can't risk that. I can't. This, the knife, it seemed like a better way. A compromise."

Harper's shoulders slumped.

"I wish you had trusted me."

I held my arms out even though I knew it was a futile offer. "I wish I had, too. I know it isn't an excuse but you were so angry, so broken after…" I trailed off, unsure how to phrase it all.

"After Samir killed my brother, destroyed my home, and tortured me?"

I felt like the worst kind of friend, the worst kind of coward. Only the length of the bed stood between us but a chasm had opened in our friendship and I wasn't sure what would close it, or if I had the strength in me to bridge it at all.

"I'm sorry," I said. Tears stung my eyes but I blinked them back. I didn't want her to think I was crying because I was sorry for myself, for being caught in the lie. "I should have told you."

Harper stood, stiff and still, for a very long time. Alek remained tense midway between us, watchful but unmoving as well. Every second of silence was another wound in my heart until I felt as though I would either bleed to death inside or start screaming just to break the tension.

"I accept your apology," Harper said after what felt like eternity and a half. She slumped onto the bed. "Do the twins know?"

"No," I muttered, relief and regret churning my stomach.

"You are going to tell them." Harper raised her eyebrows but her tone made it clear that wasn't a question.

"Yes," I said. "I should have told you all long ago. I'm truly sorry. I was just trying..."

"Nope. Shut the excuse closet, Jade. I accepted your apology but we're not okay yet. We've got bigger fucking problems though, it sounds like. But you gotta stop thinking you know what is best for everyone around you because you pretty fucking clearly don't. Kenobi."

"Ouch," I said, trying to summon a smile. She had

a point and it was a sharp one. "We do have problems," I added, glad for the distraction of current events to get us onto a less painful subject.

"You wouldn't wake up," Harper said. The anger in her face and voice had mostly faded and she looked tired. "Alek called Vivian when you wouldn't wake up this morning. We've been trying all day."

"All day?" I said. I looked at the blinds and then to the other side of the bed where the clock was. It was nearly seven. I had thought that meant it was morning but I realized the dot indicating AM or PM on the clock was firmly in the PM spot.

"I brought you home yesterday," Alek said. He looked more relaxed now that Harper no longer looked like she wanted to kill me. "I thought you were exhausted from all the magic, the way you are sometimes. I let you sleep."

"All day?" I said again. I couldn't really fault him. After I did a lot of magic I was often tired and could sleep through a whole day pretty easily. Alek had no way of knowing this was different.

"When you still had not roused this afternoon I tried to wake you," Alek said. He knelt beside the bed and caught one of my hands in his own. "You were so still," he murmured. "Still and cold. It was not natural. I knew something was wrong."

So it probably had been him calling out to me in the dream. But I had been under for hours. I recalled the wrapped in gauze, locked in feeling of the trap nightmare. Mystery sorcerer must have needed, as best I could guess, time to break into my mind, to get through natural and magical defenses. I knew very little about mind magic. My own power lent itself far better to fireballs and external expression.

"Johnny, Halfheart, his body was a trap. I got infected by the magic, I think." I pushed my own magic through my body, closing my eyes as I focused. I felt no trace of the mystery sorcerer's magic, no hint of cotton-candy sticky sweetness. Opening my eyes, I continued, "He broke into my mind through my dreams. He knows that I didn't kill Samir, that I have his heart stashed somewhere. I think I kept him from figuring out where. I didn't have my talisman in my dream and I don't think he was inside my head enough to realize why I was terrified by it being missing."

I hoped. If he knew I had Samir's heart on a chain around my neck, I had a feeling my neck would be the next thing he'd want to explode.

"You saw him?" Alek asked.

"No. He appeared looking like Aurelio, maybe he got Aurelio's form from my mind or maybe Johnny's mind, I dunno. But he did a shitty job cause Aurelio has no idea I have Samir's heart still."

"Who does know?" Harper asked. "You, Alek, Brie and Ciaran, I'm guessing?"

I nodded. "The Archivist, maybe Iollan." I tried to remember who I had told what and my head started aching. That's the problem with lies and secrets. Keeping track of them and what story you've told which person is a bitch.

"What about the suits?"

"The suits?" Alek asked and I remembered I hadn't had time to tell him about the NoS agents showing up yesterday.

"Maybe they know somehow." I had a guess that if they knew they'd bought the information from Noah, the vampire Archivist, somehow.

A year ago, I wouldn't have believed he'd sell information like that, I would have thought he was more or less on our side and wanting to keep Samir's heart safe and secret too. But after the not-so-simple job I'd not exactly done for him last fall, I didn't know where I stood with the vampire.

But I knew he was dangerous and that likely he didn't trust me. He'd certainly lied to me, as well.

I kept that wild speculation to myself. I doubted that even if that were the case, I'd ever get the agents to admit it. Noah in my experience wasn't the type to directly involve himself when he could pull the strings of others to get him what he wanted. If he wanted to fuck with me, he'd be well behind the scenes and two or three layers of plausible deniability away from anything going on.

I realized that I had slipped into my own thoughts as Harper explained about the visit the afternoon before. Alek gave me a patient, vaguely frustrated look.

"There wasn't time to tell you," I muttered. "Things have been a little crazy."

Alek's phone buzzed in his pocket before he could respond.

"Speak of the devil is the phrase, yes?" he said, looking up from his phone.

"Suits?" I said, confused.

"Lara. She says the agents are back and waiting in the store. She told them she would text you." Alek showed me the message.

I threw the comforter off my legs and stood up with Alek's steadying hand which I totally didn't need at all.

"Call Perky," I said to Harper before I realized she already had her phone out.

"On it," she said with a weak smile. The gulf between us was still there, but the chasm no longer looked impossible. It was a start.

"First, pants," I said, squeezing Alek's arm. "Then we'll go rescue Lara and hopefully witness a legal slaughter."

And I hoped it would be a slaughter of the verbal, paperwork-filled kind. For I had a feeling that government agents had nothing on a mountain lion with a law degree and a license to use it.

I got pants on but my dreams of seeing the special and not-so-special agents handed their asses died in the fire of Levi's ringtone on my phone.

"Sup?" I said, already walking toward the door and my shoes. Vivian had left apparently, for there was no sign of the wolf-shifter vet in the living room or kitchen.

"Is Alek with you? Can you get here quickly? Are you at the shop?" Levi's voice was breathless and panicked.

"Yes, sort of, at home," I said. "What's wrong?"

Alek and Harper had stopped politely pretending they couldn't hear Levi on the phone, their bodies going tense.

"Wolves, men, they're trying to get into the house and we're surrounded," Levi said. I heard a male voice ask him something but Levi didn't respond verbally. Then a huge crash sounded followed by the unmistakable crack of gunfire.

"We're on our way," I said.

"Hurry," Levi said. He started to say something else but the phone cut out.

"Shit."

"Are Carlos and May still with him?" Alek asked as he jammed his feet into his boots.

"They were with Levi?" I asked, shoving my phone into my pants. If they were there, likely this attack was the First's doing. Damnit.

"May is too weak to travel so Levi offered his place," Alek said. He strapped on his gun after handing me the Alpha and Omega in its sheath.

"I called Perky, she's on her way to the shop now. Says she'll bill you later." Harper joined us by the door, grabbing her own shoes. "That was gunfire. If they are already in we're never going to make it in time."

"Not if we drive," I said, a really stupid thought forming in my head. But Levi was in danger. Junebug and her unborn baby were probably there, too, given it was her home and all.

Nobody I loved was getting hurt on my watch. Not if I could help it.

"Jade," Alek said, his pale brows raised in an unasked question.

"Take the car, meet me there," I said. I didn't wait for him to answer. I threw open the door and ran out, leaping off my upper landing in a smooth motion.

Flying is easy in theory. You just have to convince your brain that breaking laws of physics is no biggie and then just not fall down. Magic coursed through my veins and I used it to push against the ground and the air, giant invisible wings holding me aloft. I used the magic to push myself higher, moving faster and faster until the world was a blur and my eyes watered from the freezing air rushing past.

I picked a straight line to Levi's shop and home, crossing Wylde in broad summer daylight, hoping speed and height would conceal the flying woman from the people below. In the end it wouldn't really matter if the whole damn world saw me. Levi and Junebug were in danger. And I hadn't saved May just to let her die to a bunch of unknown assailants.

The First had brought his war to my town and I

wasn't about to let him win any more battles here.

Levi's shop and garage were outside Wylde proper by a couple miles. I flew straight at it, buildings and trees whipping by below me. I squinted against the wind, watching for the obvious sight of Levi's shop's bright orange metal roof. His and Junebug's house was right behind the garage, tucked into a pretty stand of quaking aspen that formed a natural visual barrier between the commercial land and their private home.

The trees also did the trick for concealing anyone around the house, unfortunately. I spied the orange roof and dropped from the sky. I made the split-second decision that I'd rather approach the house on foot than risk trying to land among potential enemies. Two large SUVs were parked blocking the driveway between shop and house and, as my ears recovered from the pressure change, I heard more gunfire and shouting. At least someone was still alive. Finding my feet, magic still burning in my blood, I formed an invisible shield in front of me and raced around the side of the garage.

Levi's house was a ranch-style one level home laid out in almost an L shape. He'd built a porch around the front side. The big picture window that looked into

RIVER OF NO RETURN

the living room was smashed open and the front door hung askew on its hinges. A white man I didn't recognize at a glance lay dead in a pool of blood in front of the porch steps. As I skirted the body, a huge wolf sprang at me from where it had been crouched in the shadows of the trees.

I pivoted and thrust my shield out, swinging the magic like a blunt weapon. The wolf deflected off the shield with a crunch as it took the blow face first. The impact nearly took me off my feet but I pushed forward, letting momentum hold me upright. I didn't have time to deal with a single wolf, not when two more gunshots rang out from within the house. I let go of the shield spell and turned the power to a focused blast of flame instead.

The wolf, thrown off by the unexpected impact and likely with its jaw broken, didn't even try to dodge. The white-hot flames burned through its neck and chest and the shifter collapsed. Burning hair and flesh scent made me gag as I sprinted up the steps. I'd never get used to killing but leaving an injured opponent behind me seemed unwise. Plus Harper's accusations of being a Kenobi were still ringing in my head.

The living room, usually a place full of art and color

from Junebug's studio and Levi's Native art collecting habit, was trashed. A fight had gone down here and there was an alarming amount of blood spattered across broken pottery and torn wall hangings. A shifter wolf, half its head missing as though from a close-range shotgun blast, partially blocked the path and view into the kitchen.

I drew the Alpha and Omega, the dagger elongating to short sword length without me even having to ask or try to impose my will. There was no way to move silently through the wreckage so I settled for speed, trying not to wince as blood and other things I didn't want to think too hard about squished beneath my sneakers as I climbed over the wolf corpse.

The kitchen off the living room was empty but the hallway behind had a man with a gun. I charged him, magic shield in front of my outstretched left hand. He fired the gun, bullets ripping into the walls to either side as the shield deflected them. The impact barely slowed me. I thrust with the Alpha and Omega, not caring what part of him I hit. The sword would kill with a scratch.

The blade cut into his thigh as I smashed the magic shield upward to deflect his gun hand. The man's brown eyes met mine as we stood frozen for a second.

"No," he said, his expression a mix of shock and pain. Then he crumpled and fell backward, sprawling in the narrow hallway. Dead.

I shoved away any guilt over using the sword, for this man was trying to kill people I loved and would have killed me, but a part of me still hated the ease at which death came, the ease with which I could deal it out. It was easier when the sword turned things it killed into dust, but apparently it didn't feel like doing that today. Another reason to prefer fighting zombies, I guess. Smell and all.

I hadn't spent a lot of time in Levi's house but I knew there was a door to the house garage as well as a bathroom and then a spare bedroom in this hallway. All the doors here were shut. I used magic to push the man's body out of the way and threw open the door he'd been standing closest to.

The bedroom was empty of combatants but the huge hole where the windows used to be told the story. A human male I didn't recognize was sprawled across the doorway, his throat torn out. A giant wolf's body, its neck ripped open and its body covered in gaping wounds, lay curled in the middle of the room, almost obstructing my view of the body half beneath it. His jaws still full of wolf fur and flesh, the massive lion lay dead in front of the window, his body rent with bullet wounds, torn from bites, and a huge chunk of flesh missing from his visible flank.

I knew that lion. He'd carried me and terrified, stolen children safely away from Not Afraid's cave. He'd protected those kids, risked his life to try to save my former people.

Carlos.

I knew he was gone even as I reached to feel for a pulse. I blinked against the threat of tears. Carlos was dead. My friends might still live if the snarling coming in the window was any indication. Grieve later, I told myself. Fight now.

I skirted the bodies to get to the broken window and saw the battle beyond. Behind the house was Junebug's kiln and studio, as well as the woodpile and a wide, cleared area of browning grass. The fight had spilled out into the open there and didn't seem to be going in my friends' favor.

Junebug knelt on top of the woodpile with a rifle in her hands that I guessed was out of ammo from the way she held it like a baseball bat instead of ready to fire. May was crouched beside the kindling box in human form, bleeding from her right shoulder, a kitchen knife in her left hand. The blood on the knife said she'd made use of it.

The wolves were focused on Levi in his wolverine form, circling him as he crouched. A wolverine the size of a German Shepherd is no joke, but these were shifter wolves, which meant they in turn were more like small horses. Levi was already bleeding from a gash on his side.

I jumped through the broken window, ignoring the sting as my leg caught on some broken glass. I staggered gracelessly away from the house, managing to catch my balance, just. Purple fire encircled my left hand and blue fire lit the Alpha and Omega as the sword lengthened to long-sword form. These wolves had killed my mate's mentor and friend. They were definitely looking to kill my best friend, and likely his pregnant wife, and May also.

They picked the wrong fight and the wrong damn town.

"Hey you mangy assholes," I yelled. "Who wants to die first?"

My words did the trick of distracting the wolf-shifters away from Levi.

One of the wolves shifted and held up his hand as though that could stop me from obliterating him.

"Stop," he said. He was a tall white man with tanned skin and a confident sneer to his face I hated instantly. "Our fight is not with you. The First would like to…"

Whatever else he would have said, I didn't care. Maybe if he hadn't attacked my friends. Definitely they shouldn't have killed Carlos. The time for talking was long since as gone as the pile of bodies behind me.

I turned him into a pillar of purple flame as I strode forward. I poured out my magic recklessly, anger and grief fueling my power. Levi took the distraction as opportunity, leaping onto the nearest wolf. His jaws stripped fur from flesh.

The other wolf charged at me and launched itself into the air with a snarl. I whipped the sword up as I dodged to the side, letting go of the fire. The blade caught the wolf along the jaw, a glancing slice that with a normal weapon would have hurt but hardly deterred a shifter. Blue flames licked over the jaw and face of the wolf and it howled as it twisted away from me. The wolf fell over like someone had yelled "timber", crashing into the ground, dead where it lay.

Levi was still growling and ripping at the twitching body of the wolf he'd attacked.

"Levi," Junebug said as she scrabbled down from the woodpile. "He's dead."

"There were at least two others," May said, standing up, her eyes flicking around the yard and examining the shadows beneath the aspens. She leaned heavily on the kindling bin as though she didn't trust her legs to support her.

"Dead," I said.

"Car," Junebug said as Levi left the wolf's corpse and crouched beside her.

"Harper and Alek," I told them. I hoped I wasn't wrong. "We're back here!"

I heard a car door slam. I readied a shield just in case it wasn't friendlies. We waited, no one moving.

Alek rounded the side of the house, gun drawn but pointed toward the ground. Harper was close on his heels in her fox form.

"We got them all, I think," I called to Alek, hoping he wouldn't turn toward the house, wouldn't look through the gaping hole where the window had been and into the bedroom. Wanting to save him from grief for even seconds longer.

131

Harper shifted to human. "Vivian should be behind us soon, she was grabbing some first aid shit."

Alek slid his gun into the holster and his shoulders relaxed. I willed the Alpha and Omega back to dagger form and put it away as I walked toward him. I'd almost reached Alek when he looked around again and then down at me.

"Where is Carlos?" he said softly and I knew no matter how much I loved him, there were some kinds of pain from which I could never protect him.

"He died saving me," May said. She didn't even wince as Vivian put another stitch in the wound in her shoulder.

Vivian had come behind Harper and Alek, and Sheriff Lee showed up not long after. The gunfire had been called in, but the sheriff had been able to deflect human interest in it after Vivian called her on her way over and gave her the quick scoop on the situation as she knew it. Rachel said she'd write Levi up for testing a new gun out without giving the office warning and that would be that.

Which still left a pile of bodies and a lot of pain.

Alek had carried Carlos' body out of the house to the

stand of trees, and covered it in a bright yellow and green quilt Junebug gave to him. My mate had pushed me away gently with a sad shake of his head and I left him to stand guard over his friend. It was a sign of Alek's grief that he hadn't even noticed the deep cut on my thigh where I'd lacerated myself with the window glass, but part of me was glad for his distraction.

I hadn't been as lucky with Vivian who had insisted on cleaning the already healing wound and making sure all the glass fragments were out. May hadn't been lucky either. Apparently her snow leopard form had taken a few bullets and she couldn't shift to heal since her other half needed to heal, so she was getting good old fashioned stitches for the moment. Since the house was a disaster zone of corpses, we were in Levi's office off of his shop and garage.

"He was a protector," I said, trying to find the words and knowing that nothing would be adequate. I'd barely known Carlos. "He'd be glad you lived." I felt in my bones that was true from everything I'd seen of him.

The dark grey rings around May's irises had expanded, pressing the golden-brown inner ring to a single band around her pupils. Pain was etched in her face, the kind of pain that went beyond physical wounds.

"All for nothing," she murmured. "Because a madman wants us dead."

"And that madman failed," I said, hollow as the words sounded. But I couldn't let her sink into despair, not now. The First was firing shots, his people had come to my town, hurt my people. This might be a shifter war in the making, but now the bastard had poked the dragon, kind of literally.

"Freyda is on her way," Rachel said from the doorway. She'd stepped out into the garage to make a few calls. "She's bringing people to help clean up."

"May needs to rest. Levi, too. I'd tell Jade to rest but she's going to ignore me," Vivian said, handing out glares to all of us.

Levi was back in human form, one arm in a sling and the other curled around Junebug's shoulders. They were cuddled into an overstuffed paisley chair that had seen better days sometime back in the seventies. Levi just nodded at the vet, which showed how tired he was.

"Not letting him go anywhere yet," Junebug said with a wan smile.

I tested my leg and found it ached but was just fine

for the basics like standing and walking. My jeans were another matter but there wasn't much I could do about the rips and bloodstains at the moment. At least my phone had survived for once. Score a point for buying the most robust, basic cell phone and case I could find. Advertising for it said it could live through an apocalypse. I hoped I'd never test that.

Harper was outside, pacing. I felt her frustration. There was very little either of us could do at the moment.

"Hey," I said. I stood awkwardly in the shadow of the building, feeling like a teenager who has just learned they have hands and doesn't know where to put them while they talk to the cool new kid at school. The bedroom, our conversation about Samir, it all felt like weeks ago even though it wasn't even hours yet.

"You ok?" Harper asked, looking me over.

"Yeah, just a flesh wound," I said, trying to get a smile out of her.

"It's going to get worse, isn't it?" she said. She had an expression like somehow this was my fault, though I knew intellectually I was probably reading way too much into it.

I was saved from having to answer by the arrival of

Freyda and her wolves. They came in two trucks. Freyda got out of the driver's side of one truck and waved a greeting as Rachel came out of the shop behind us.

"I want you to look at the bodies," the sheriff said, not wasting pleasantries or time. "See if you recognize anyone from your run-in the other day."

Harper and I followed Rachel and Freyda as her pack started pulling tarps and ropes from the trucks.

"This one," Freyda said as we reached the human male lying in the pool of blood by the porch steps. "This was the one who forced us to shift. I think he was the leader."

"Good thing they shot him first," Harper said. "Junebug is pregnant," she added as we all gave her questioning looks.

"Levi told you then?" I said, relieved that I wouldn't have to worry about slipping up and mentioning it. Harper was right, if this guy had forced Junebug to shift, it would have killed the baby.

"Of course he did. He's my friend. Friends tell each other important things," Harper said. She glared at me and walked back toward the trucks without another word.

Oof. I'd walked into that one face first. Apparently we weren't okay yet.

"At least we got the leader," I said, trying to diffuse the weird tension. I ignored the look that Freyda and Rachel exchanged.

"Let's go take a look at the rest and figure out how to handle making all this go away," Freyda said. Her smile was understanding and gentle and I suddenly couldn't handle either at the moment.

"I'm going to go check on Alek," I said. I walked away from them and circled the house, taking deep, calming breaths.

Part of it was uncertainty with Harper, I knew. Part was that I was exhausted still. I'd been burning magic like it was going out of style, I'd not gotten proper rest thanks to that damn sorcerer fucking up shifters in the woods and hunting Samir's heart, and everything happening seemed to be pointing toward more battles to come. To think, a week before I'd been almost bored. Grass is always greener right?

I found Alek kneeling beside Carlos' covered body, his blond head bowed as though in prayer or deep contemplation. When he raised his face as I walked up to him, I saw his bloodshot eyes were the color of a winter sky—desolate and empty of all warmth. Ignoring the sharp pain in my leg, I dropped to my knees beside him and wound my fingers through his. His hand was even cold despite the warm evening air.

"I should have been here," Alek said.

"What would you tell me? That we can't save everyone? He died saving May. Saving Junebug and her baby, and Levi too."

"It is one thing to know with the head, and another our hearts." Alek squeezed my hand and I felt some of the warmth return to his gaze as he turned his head to look into my eyes. "He raised me from an idiot teenager to be a Justice, to be a man. He saved me many times. Now he is gone and I can do nothing."

I tugged gently on his hand, pulling him so his weight leaned into me a little. Reminding him the only way I knew how that he wasn't alone. He tucked his head against mine with a heavy sigh.

"Freyda is here," I said after a moment. "Whenever you are ready."

Alek nodded. We knelt, side by side, hand in hand, and held a quiet vigil for his dead friend.

ANNIE BELLET

We buried Carlos in a stand of silver and green-leafed trees on Levi's land. Freyda's pack had wrapped up and taken away the other bodies. The only sign of the fight left was blood stains, a boarded-up window, and a handful of grieving shifters leaning on each other in the darkness.

"Freyda's offered to put us all up at The Den," Levi told me. He still had his arm around Junebug, the two of them apparently glued together since the fight.

Not that I blamed them. I didn't want to let go of Alek's arm, and not just because both of us were exhausted.

"We have a guest room," I said.

I wished I'd thought of that before, at Vivian's, so that Carlos and May had been staying with us. If they had, Carlos might have lived. I pushed the thought away. If they had, it's possible that someone else might have died. Lara or Harper or Alek... There are no sadder, more useless words in any language than "what if" and "if only." Dwelling on them would drive anyone mad.

Levi shook his head. "No offense, but I'd feel safer at the Den. Though staying above the shop would be awesome."

140

"No offense taken," I said. "I could be arrested by a secret government agency or something any day now anyway."

Saying that of course caused a lot of other questions, which I answered as best I could, not mentioning the magic door that Samir had shipped me from beyond the grave. Well, the almost grave. If being a ruby-like lump stuck in a talisman around your killer's neck was grave-equivalent.

May was also going with Levi and Junebug, under protests that it was too dangerous for her to remain that were immediately glared down by everyone around her. I had a sinking feeling that nowhere was going to be very safe soon. Danger to the right of us, danger to the left of us, and all that jazz.

"You are welcome at the Den also," Freyda told Alek and me.

I was surprised at the sincerity in her voice considering the two times I'd been in her Great Hall things had gone explosive. She wasn't making the offer out of politeness but instead looked like a resigned and determined commander who was girding herself for war.

"I have to go meet my lawyer," I said. Perky had

sent me two messages that read very polite but insistent in their undertone and the fact that there were two of them when she wasn't the type to waste time like that.

We said our farewells. Alek and May had a few quiet words as he helped her into Freyda's SUV. Harper said she'd walk home from the game store so she tagged along with us. It was a quiet, awkward ride back.

Lara had closed up the store for me. I made probably my hundredth mental note to give her a raise soon. She was practically a partner in my shop with how much time she spent there lately and with how much I'd come to rely on her. The building was mostly dark except the upper outside light shining on my landing. Summer's deluge of bugs danced in the beam of light and Aurelio waited patiently in the glow.

Aurelio ignored my invitation to sit as he followed Harper, Alek, and I into my living room after an amusing, at least to my exhausted brain, shuffle of bodies as everyone tried to remove their shoes before coming into the apartment proper. I supposed I should have put in a better foyer or something. Alek didn't sit either, instead looming near me, his face lined with grief and wariness. Harper perched on the edge of one of the armchairs. Though it felt a little rude, I slumped onto my couch with a heavy sigh. I was out of energy for standing and my couch cushions felt like seductive clouds begging me to rest.

"Three of my pack members are going after the

sorcerer," Aurelio said. He ran a hand through his dark hair, which stood up enough despite its shaggy length that it was obvious he'd spent a lot of the day repeating the gesture.

"That is stupid," Alek said. I glanced at him. He was definitely out of fucks to give if he was being that blunt right out the gate. I could relate.

"He's not wrong," I said.

"I couldn't talk them out of it," Aurelio said in a tone that implied he had definitely made more than one attempt to do so.

"The man who did that to your pack member is a sorcerer," I said. "But he's not interested in you. I think it was a way to get to me. He's got some kind of mind magic."

Closing my eyes I leaned into the couch and took a deep breath. I hadn't had the time to face what happened at the Den. I'd been too busy fighting with Harper and then fighting for my friends' lives. I still had to deal with the government dudes and find out from Perky how that went and there was no telling when the First would make another move, though I hoped killing all his minions would at least give him some pause before he fucked with my town again.

Alek's hands settled onto my shoulders as he moved around the back of the couch. He gave me a gentle squeeze.

"I know they can't fight a sorcerer alone," Aurelio said. "Especially not one who can sever us somehow. But I cannot stop them from trying." He said the last words slowly but with great force as though they hurt to get out.

I opened my eyes and met his bleak gaze. I knew what it felt like to have the people I loved determined to fight something they didn't understand and couldn't beat.

"I will talk to them," Alek said. He held up a hand to forestall Aurelio's response as the other man shook his head. "To talk them out of it. The sorcerer wants something Jade has. He will come to us. It is wiser to wait and fight on known ground."

On ground that was full of people I cared about. On ground full of innocent bystanders. What kind of damage would a sorcerer who could sever shifters from their other selves and cause them to explode do in a town full of shifters and far-more-vulnerable humans? Aurelio had said something about the guy having human back-up, humans with guns. Universe knew that men with guns could be destructive enough on their own, even without magic backing them up.

"I was not clear," Aurelio started to say.

All three shifters' heads swiveled toward the door and a moment later I heard the clang of footsteps on the metal stairs.

"Relax," I said. "It's probably just my lawyer." I had texted Kate Perkins, aka Perky, as we pulled onto our street, not realizing at that point that I already had company.

Alek got the door and Kate entered with raised eyebrows as she took in the scene. I thought about standing but the lead formerly known as my muscles talked me out of it. Aurelio's nostrils flared and then he relaxed as his senses must have told him the impeccably dressed blonde bombshell in front of him was a shifter, too. Kate's perfectly arched eyebrows crept a little higher.

"Didn't realize you'd have company," she said as she kicked off her heels.

"Kate Perkins, meet Aurelio, also known as Softpaw, Alpha of the Bitterroot pack. Aurelio, my lawyer, Kate." I managed a smile as I waved a hand back and forth.

Kate inclined her head and walked into the living room. She sat on the chair Harper wasn't leaning against and set her dark pink leather briefcase onto the coffee table.

"We will go," Alek said, giving Aurelio and Harper a stern look. "Talk to Softpaw's pack. I will return."

Aurelio looked frustrated as he shook his head again, as though he thought Alek's chance of persuading the pack was no better. If their own Alpha couldn't convince them, a man they appeared to obey without a lot of questions from what I'd seen, I doubted my mate, no matter how awesome and Justice-y he could be, would have better luck. Especially not in his current mood.

Which made what I was about to say even harder to put into words. I had a feeling I was about to piss off my mate. But hey, I'd already alienated my best friend, what was one more fight with someone I loved?

Because I knew what I had to do. And it sucked, but we were just running around putting out fires. If I'd learned anything from my years of struggle and the final battles with Samir, it was that eventually you run out of water.

"No," I said, putting as much finality into the word

as I could. "I'll go with you, Aurelio. You can't fight him, but I can." I hoped. I was hella tired but with a night of sleep and a hot meal in me, miracles were possible.

"No," Alek said. "This looks like trap." His accent thickened as he paced toward me.

"Normally I'm all for a fight, but seriously, Jade. I agree with the tiger," Harper said, breaking the silence she'd held the entire way home in the car and up to this point. "You'd be taking exactly what he wants right to him." She stared pointedly at my chest.

I resisted the urge to tuck my talisman under my teeshirt as I shook my head.

"Yes," I said. "Technically. But fighting battles on multiple fronts is just wearing us out and meanwhile more people are going to get hurt or die. If the mind-trick sorcerer comes here, he'll have a whole town full of shifters he could sever and humans he could use or destroy. We know where he is, or at least where he was as of a couple days ago. We take the fight to him, eliminate that threat." It had sounded less crazy in my head, but not by much.

"I'm going to pretend I'm not hearing you planning murder, so don't mind me," Kate said. She leaned back in the chair looking almost amused.

I decided not to tell her that I'd killed multiple people before breakfast.

"For fuck's sake," I tried again. "I have to even designate which sorcerer we are talking about, that's how screwed things are. I'm going after mind-guy before the First has the chance to recover from today and send more assholes at us. We know where mind-guy is," I repeated. "He's an enemy we can fight."

Aurelio cleared his throat. "Are you all finished?" he asked.

"Tell your pack members to wait and I'll go, you can show me where," I said. "After I sleep."

"They already left."

"Wait, what? Why didn't you say that?" It did explain why he was here. He truly needed my help and his words only strengthened my resolve to take care of this latest fire once and for fucking all.

Aurelio just raised his eyebrows and even Alek had the presence of mind to look a bit sheepish. We'd been arguing what to do without even listening. In our defense, it had been a horrible no good very bad day.

"He's deep in the Frank," Aurelio said. "At an old logging camp. I think he knows about the druid since

ANNIE BELLET

it is out of his normal range," he added with a glance at Kate.

"Hopefully he doesn't know the druid is on his honeymoon," I said. I tried not to think about how convenient it was that Brie, Ciaran, and Iollan, three of my more powerful friends and allies, were all out of the action. The last time something like that happened, we'd all nearly died by Samir's doing.

I gave in and gripped my talisman, reassuring myself that Samir's heart gem was still safely in the one spot on the D20.

"This is a terrible idea," Alek said again. His blue eyes were like bruises in his exhausted face.

"I'm going with you," Harper said.

I started to open my mouth to object to that but saw the set of her jaw and the hardness in her eyes. My heart ached but I knew there was zero chance of talking her out of it. Alek gave her a look that was probably similar to Caesar's when Brutus stabbed him.

"Fine," he said in a tone that said the opposite. "In morning."

Aurelio's shoulders slumped but he had the good sense not to push it. He likely could tell we were all at the end of our ropes. "We'll leave at dawn. It's a long hike. Longer on human feet. They have a head start tonight but knowing them, they will not attack the camp immediately, so we might be able to catch up."

"Meet here?" I asked.

He nodded. Alek growled but held his tongue as Aurelio took the hint and left quickly. Harper slid into the armchair with a look that challenged any of us to tell her to leave. Nobody took her up on that challenge.

"It is a trap," Alek said. He sat rigidly on the couch beside me, his thigh hard and warm against my own, the tension making both of us vibrate slightly.

"Good thing I'm a badass," I said, tugging on his arm until he settled back beside me.

Alek's look told me just how unconvincing I was curled here on the couch probably looking just as worn out as I felt.

"That fire is dealt with," I said, looking at Kate. "What have you got for me?"

"They aren't going to give us privacy, are they?" Kate said.

"Nope," Harper said. "We can hear anything in the apartment anyway."

Alek just peeled his lips back from his teeth in response.

"Ignore them," I said. "How did it go with the agents?" I almost apologized for leaving her hanging like that but caught myself in time. She had probably been glad I wasn't there to inadvertently muck it up by saying something stupid.

"They are out for your blood, but they don't have shit. They are desperate to find some guy named Samir," she said. "They didn't come out and say it, but I got the impression they think you killed him."

"I didn't kill him," I said, more or less truthfully. I kept my eyes on Kate and deliberately away from Harper's face. It felt like I was salting the wounds my secrets had opened for Harper, but she'd insisted on staying.

"Well, that's a relief," Kate said in the bubbly, slyly sarcastic tone that had helped earn her the nickname Perky. She pulled her phone out of her briefcase and swiped it on before holding it out to me. "Do you recognize this?"

I took the phone. On the screen was a picture of a small but ornate skeleton key. It could have been any key, really. Except, it wasn't. I recognized the shape of it, the almost heart-shaped back of the key, the delicate filigree, the rainbow sheen to the dark metal.

"Yes," I said after a moment. I was pretty sure my face had already given that away even if I had been inclined to lie to my lawyer, which I wasn't. "It's Samir's." From the picture, it looked like the key was resting on some kind of plastic bag. Evidence bag. Shit.

"You sold it?" Kate asked.

"What?" I said. "No. I haven't seen it in almost thirty years. Is that an evidence bag?"

"The agents tried to give me the run around at first, but like I said, they are desperate for some reason. So they let me photograph this and told me they had a witness who said you sold it to him."

"Witness is lying," I said, handing Kate back her phone. I leaned into Alek, hating the tension still rippling through him.

"It's thin evidence of anything even so," she said. "They can't prove he kept it on him or that he didn't give it to you or someone as a gift."

I bit back a response to that. There was zero way Samir would have given that key to anyone. It had once been the key to a lock around my damn neck. Someone was setting me up and I had a suspicion as to who would have the access, knowledge, and power to do so.

I also knew that Noah Grey, the Archivist, would never be stupid enough to reveal himself. He'd have used middle men. If I was right, the question was why? I'd pissed him off, but this much? Still, this had the feel of him, somehow. Coming at me from the shadows, sideways. Noah was one of the few people on the planet who knew I hadn't killed Samir but was keeping his heart somewhere. Fortunately for us, the vampire had no idea where or how, as far as I knew.

"Jade?" Kate said and I realized I'd been silently staring into space for a good while.

"I'm sorry," I said. "We're exhausted and I can't deal with this right now if I don't have to."

"You don't have to," she said with a gentle smile. "This is what you pay me the big bucks for. They'll want an interview but I can put them off. Though you disappearing for a hike in the wilderness won't look good."

"Tell them it was a prior commitment that I can't get out of and I'll talk to them next week," I said, managing a smile.

"I'll do what I do," she said.

"Thanks, Kate," I added.

"I thought y'all called me Perky," she said as her smile widened.

Harper snorted and I shook my head, returning her grin. "Only in my head and almost never aloud," I said.

Harper made a coughing sound that came out suspiciously like the word bullshit and I mock-glared at her. She'd coined the damn nickname. I had a feeling that Perky knew that we also called her partner, Harrison Smitt, "Smitten."

"I like it," she said as she made her way to the door.

"She's kinda amazing," Harper said after Perky had left. "I'm taking the guest bed. Don't you even think about leaving without me," she added with a glare.

"Wouldn't dream of it," I said. I winced, recalling the spell-induced dreams I'd been stuck in. I didn't feel the cotton-candy magic or catch any sign of it, hadn't since I'd awoken, but now I was afraid to sleep.

Alek paced the living room and shook his head when I pointed out a shower might be wise for both of us.

"What if I cannot protect you?" he murmured softly in Russian.

So. There it was. I stepped into his embrace and pressed my cheek to his chest. He'd lost someone he loved today and now I was running headlong into danger, danger he couldn't kill for me. Another enemy he couldn't fight. My tired brain refused to find non-stupid-sounding words to tell him I understood so I just clung to him, breathing in his scent, letting him breathe in mine.

"You must rest, kitten," he said after what felt like not nearly long enough.

"I don't know if I can," I whispered.

"Try," came his murmured response. "Please try."

My body was of the Yoda school where there was no try. Stumbling into our bedroom, I decided a shower could wait until morning. I'd cleaned up some at Levi's though it felt woefully inadequate. I pulled off my clothes and crashed as soon as my head hit the pillow. I barely registered that Alek didn't come to bed at all.

13

There's nothing like jogging through the woods with a bunch of shifters to make me glad I'd been keeping up on my cardio by doing runs with Alek a few mornings a week. I focused on my breathing and not tripping over fir tree roots and thought about how only a few years ago my idea of working out was not using the fast travel in Skyrim. Aurelio's pack fanned out around us, the huge shifter-wolves often invisible in the trees. Aurelio stayed near, in his wolf form once we'd gotten away from town. Harper had shifted to her fox form but Alek remained in his human one, his long legs easily and gracefully putting the miles behind him.

I'd made myself eat a three-egg omelet and two

pieces of toast after waking up feeling not exactly refreshed. We'd set out as the sun was rising, turning the sky the color of raw meat pink and gun-metal grey. The morning was still but had a heaviness that promised early summer heat later. For the first part of our journey, we were under the thick canopy of Douglas firs but as the ground rose in elevation the fir trees started to give way to Ponderosa pines and the occasional spruce. The heat shimmered on expanses of exposed rock as we stopped at the mouth of a canyon, the wolves testing the air with their noses.

I took the chance to drink from the canteen I'd brought in my backpack then rolled my shoulders to work out the stiffness. I offered the water to Alek and he drank a couple sips without saying anything. He'd been quiet all morning and I was saving all my breath for the journey. I had no idea what to say, anyway. Grief is monster that takes a different shape for each of us, and often it is a beast we must wrestle alone until we are ready.

Aurelio shifted to human. "We must climb up the canyon I think," he said, motioning to the steep, rocky slope ahead.

Lichens and grasses clung to deposits of soil but few

trees found purchase. The ground was open and we'd be obvious moving along it. The floor of the canyon, where a mostly dry stream trickled through boulders and slabs of stone, was choked with sagebrush and bearberry. I could see why we wouldn't want to go that way, none of us had anything to cut the brush and it would be very slow going.

"How close are we?" I asked.

"I am not sure," Aurelio said. "We came a somewhat different path perhaps, for this should look more familiar but does not. However, I was carrying Halfheart. It is hard to remember when much of our travel was in the dark, but we found Bird and Snowdrop's scents. They left a trail, knowing I would follow. This is the way. It is still some miles to the old camp, I think."

"They going to be okay?"

"Bird is an ambusher. He fought in one of your wars," Aurelio said with a shrug that was deceptively casual considering the tension radiating from him. "I do not think he will do something stupid like a frontal assault. Snowdrop would not let him. Always Singing is young, he idolizes Bird, so he will do whatever Bird does."

I realized that Always Singing was the name of the

third mutineer in Aurelio's pack just in time to not look like an idiot asking what he meant by that.

"Lead the way," I said. "We should stop again once you recognize any landmarks so we can try to come up with a better plan than charge in, magic blazing." I attempted a grin and from Aurelio's amused snort must have been somewhat successful.

Alek did not look amused. I knew he still felt this was a trap but so far there had been no sign of trouble. There had been no sign of anything unless squirrels and birds counted. I put my canteen away, shouldered my backpack again, and started after Aurelio and the pack.

The side of the canyon was steep but we were able to forge a path zig-zagging our way along the side. Out from under the trees on the hillside the air grew hotter, the sun was unrelenting. I focused on putting one foot in front of the other, knowing that I was unlikely to hear or see any danger before my preternatural companions would.

We had climbed along the canyon far enough that the sun was dropping, the shadows cast by the larger chunks of grey and brown stone changing their direction. Above us was a stand of trees, their own shadows stretching out like seeking fingers over the ground. Alek paused behind me.

"We're close," he said in a low voice. "I can smell them."

Aurelio and his wolves were fanned out around us on the slope, most of them farther along and higher up. They were sniffing the air as our whole party stopped. The steep hillside was quiet other than our movement, no sign of humans or even a squirrel. The tension of knowing there would be a fight soon was getting to us. Taking a step, I caught my hiking boot on a chunk of stone and stumbled, putting my hands out to catch myself on a large, lichen-covered rock to my left.

My arms went right through the stone and hit cloth. Cotton-candy scent, strong as if I'd been at the County Fair eating a cloud of it, filled my nose as whatever I'd fallen on moved.

"Danger," I yelled as I summoned my magic. I pushed myself off the man in fatigues as he rose straight out of the illusory stone.

He had a gun in his hands and there was no time for finesse. I slammed a wave of force into him, sending him tumbling back. I heard gun shots and yelps as other hidden men rose up around us. Higher up on the slope ahead of us, in the stand of fir trees, I caught the glint of metal and more bodies moving in the shadows. A wave of cotton-candy magic shimmered down the slope and I met it with the biggest shield I could manifest.

Aurelio and the pack scattered across the hillside trying to reach the half-hidden gunmen. Alek had shifted to his tiger form and charged down toward two men who were trying to shoot us from behind. I couldn't see where Harper was, her brown-red coat and smaller body blending too perfectly into the landscape.

The ground beneath us began to shake. Then to rumble. Directly above where Alek and I were was a steeper portion of the canyon wall. As I fought to maintain a shield around us and move forward toward the trees, the canyon-side gave way.

"Move," I screamed. I tried to grab Alek with a tentacle of magic, thinking I could fly us up above the landslide rumbling toward us but a huge wall of dirt and debris shot up between us as though forced by invisible wind.

Illusion. I knew it was an illusion but I couldn't see

beyond it. I had no idea where Alek was. I turned and funneled all my power into a shield, bracing as the ground slid beneath my feet. A boulder the size of Alek's truck slammed into my shield. The force and weight of it pushed me back and I stepped onto ground no longer beneath me. The rock and earth piling up on my magic shield wasn't an illusion at all.

I fell backward. Alek emerged from the swirling debris. He was about twenty feet away and barely protected by the shield holding back the landslide. The earth beneath me started to run as though it was water, pushing me farther and farther down the hill. I had to fly but I was terrified that I'd lose the shield and all that rock and earth would bury Alek as he fought to keep his footing and reach me.

"No, go back," I tried to tell him but the unnatural wind pushing stinging debris between us ripped my words away.

I wasn't sure I could manage three spells at once but I had to try. I pushed myself away from the ground a good ten feet into the air, and felt the shield buckle as I redirected my will to stay over the tumbling earth. Then I formed a tentacle, picturing it like an extension of my arm as I reached out and tried to wrap my magic around Alek.

My shield failed as another boulder, this one easily house sized, slammed into it with unnatural force. For a moment I lost my concentration as cotton-candy magic whipped the dust and gravel to skin-removing levels and the tide of earth and stone broke the magic dam and rumbled toward me. Something slammed into my shoulder and a wound bloomed as blood gushed. The pain was immediate and burning.

A bullet wound. I'd been shot enough to know. With my shield down it wasn't just the hillside crashing toward us that I had to fear. Another bullet grazed my thigh, tearing a bloody, burning path. The shot pushed me around and I dropped down into the churning path of the landslide.

I lost the hold I'd had on Alek. I wrapped my magic around me in the best shield I could manage as the world went dark and loud. I tried to push myself upward with more magic but I wasn't sure which way that was as I was knocked around like a pinball. Stone and earth and broken vegetation battered my shield, carrying me along. The sorcerer's magic coated all of it; he was pushing the rockslide to pick up more debris, to go faster, unnaturally enhancing an already overwhelming force.

I closed my eyes and focused every ounce of power

I could muster on not being crushed.

It wasn't enough. I couldn't breathe. My shield was hit over and over and over. Every blow absorbed, deflected. But I didn't know which way was up, which way was out. I tried to stop the panic that formed as I was tumbled like a piece of sea glass in a wave.

Then it stopped and a great weight settled on me. I opened my eyes and blinked at the grit that filtered into my lashes. Darkness.

Darkness and no air. The weight increased. I poured magic into my shield and tried to shove upward, outward. To move the tons of dirt and rock.

No air. No movement. I might as well have tried to use my magic to move the planet Earth itself for all the good it did. I wasn't sure I was facing upward. I could have been shoving against the ground for all I could tell. I tried to calm my heart, to calm my breathing. My shoulder was a mass of aching pressure, my thigh a searing throb.

Don't panic.

Focus on the shield. Don't get crushed.

Don't panic. Focus.

No air.

Then… only darkness.

14

I awoke in a hospital room. The bed was angled slightly upright. There was a window with the curtains drawn to one side and a chair to the other. Alek sat in the chair, his eyes closed as though he had fallen asleep while keeping vigil. I was wearing scrubs and had a blue knit blanket part way covering my legs. I looked down at my arm, seeing the IV needle taped there. Some kind of monitoring machine was next to the IV bag but it was turned off. The air had an antiseptic tinge to it and a chill that failed to raise goosebumps on my exposed skin. I shifted experimentally on the bed. My shoulder and thigh felt fine. Nothing looked like it was bandaged.

"Jade," Alek said. "You're awake. Finally. How do you feel?"

"Fine, but we have to go now, before that asshole gets the heart," I said.

I ripped the IV needle from my arm. A bead of blood formed where it left my skin but I didn't even feel a sting. There was a single door into the room. It had a plastic bin on the back of it with a folder tucked into it. There was writing on a white label on the folder, but I couldn't read it from where I lay. The floor was speckled tile that a designer on HGTV would probably call eggshell.

"Wait," Alek said. He rose, his body tense and his face etched with alarm. "What do you mean?"

"The cowardly pickledicked bastard," I said. My feet were bare and the tiles felt cold beneath them as I stood up. "The one who buried me under the rockslide. He's going for the heart. We have to make sure it is safe."

Alek seemed to be having trouble processing this. He grabbed my shoulders and pushed me back into the bed.

"You aren't well. Tell me where it is and I'll check. You need more rest."

"It's right here, asshole," I said as I punched him in the throat.

Not-Actually-Alek reeled back and I charged past him, throwing open the hospital room door. I knew two things now.

One, that the asshole who had dropped a mountainside on me had spent more time in hospital rooms than I ever had given how much detail he'd put into this illusion.

Two, that we were definitely not in Idaho anymore. I wasn't sure if it was a dreamscape like before, or perhaps some kind of mental construction where he'd trapped my unconscious mind, but this wasn't the real world.

Outside the door was a hallway that stretched into dimness in either direction. Not-Alek lunged for me and I kicked him back. I reached for magic but wasn't surprised to find no response.

Not in the box. Out of the box, I told myself. This wasn't real. There was no "there" there.

A sword appeared in my hand even as I visualized it and not-Alek scrambled back as I turned on him swinging.

"I can see you have no appreciation for finesse," he

said. "Make this easy, Jade, tell me what I want to know and I'll leave you in peace."

"You dropped a fucking hillside on me," I said. I tried not to imagine anyone else stuck beneath the rocks. Harper had been out of range, as had Aurelio and most of the other wolves. But Alek... I pushed away that thought. Despair wouldn't serve me now.

"You won't save yourself by playing games with me," the asshole said. The hospital room faded away and we stood on a hillside now that looked much like the one I'd been fighting him on.

I thought about burgers and the scene changed to the street outside Marnie's grill. Not-Alek looked pissed and the hillside returned. So... we were inside my mind and I had some control here. Good to know.

"Why do you think I have Samir's heart?" I asked him as I lunged forward, thrusting with the sword.

A shield appeared on his arm and he blocked the blow, his simulation of Alek's face twisted with frustration.

"You already revealed you did," he said. "You reveal more than you think. No one's mind is uncrackable, given enough time. And we have all the time. My snipers can hold your people in this canyon until they starve if I want them to."

So my people were still alive. I hoped that meant Alek, too. The image of Alek laying on the cement outside my shop, a hole through his neck, slammed into me as the hillside gave way to cement. Tires screeched as the SUV with the wolves who had shot him peeled away.

Just a memory. Dangerous. I charged at not-Alek as he sat up from the ground, his throat a gaping wound.

"Tell me," not-Alek said, blood dripping down his shirt. "And I'll let this one go." He motioned to himself.

The landscape changed around us again as I processed what he'd said. Alek was alive, at least that's what my tormentor was insinuating. Without thinking, I reached for my talisman with my free hand but found nothing around my neck.

The world blurred. We stood now in a field surrounded by trees. Samir stood not even twenty feet in front of me, blood running down his arm.

"Traitors," Samir hissed.

Shit. Memory again. Burning fog rose in tendrils from the ground.

"Show me," not-Alek murmured at my side.

"No." I thought about the hillside rushing down on

me, about my fear for Alek, the feel of rock and gravel and dirt burying me alive.

Hillside again, Samir's face and the burning fog disappeared.

I morphed the sword to a laser sword and unleashed on not-Alek with a flurry of attacks. We danced across the rocky bottom of the canyon, my sword slicing and dicing sage brush and starting tiny fires. The too-still air took on the scent of burning brush, but faint for how much vegetation was smoking now, as though the mindscape was more echo and afterthought of what reality should be than anything truly tangible.

The fact that he was dodging told me that attacking in this place still meant something, was potentially dangerous to him. Otherwise why would he bother? I visualized a spike of rock shooting up at him from the ground. Not-Alek leapt into the air just before I manifested the earth spike as though he could anticipate my very thoughts.

Which, given he was invading my mind, made a sick kind of sense.

I dropped a twenty-ton anvil on him. No visualization this time, I just went with the first image that came into my head. No delay between thought and manifestation.

The anvil crashed into the asshole and slammed him into the ground.

The air and light went out of the world for a moment as my chest felt like it was being crushed from all sides. Cotton-candy strands wrapped around me, brushing my hands, arms, and face like spider webs. I tried to gasp, to choke, to move at all.

Then I was back on the hillside. The sage was whole again, no smoke hung in the air. I fell to my knees, coughing, even though I told myself it wasn't real.

Clapping sounded behind me as not-Alek picked his way across the rocks toward me.

"Was that fun?" he said, his mouth twisting in an unattractive way that Alek's never would.

"You have real talent," I said, spitting what was probably imaginary grit from my mouth. The dirt tasted real enough, like sand on my teeth and lips. "You're in the shape of one of the hottest people I've ever met, and you still manage to look ugly and pathetic. How do you do it?"

Maybe not the smartest plan to insult someone who was clearly holding my brain hostage, but if it kept me far away from any memories of Samir, I was okay with that. What was inappropriately timed snark for if not saving lives?

"How long do you think you can last under that much rock and dirt? You won't die, of course. Dying isn't for our kind. But this won't be a comfortable undeath. You can make it stop anytime." Not-Alek's eyes were cold and he folded his arms across his chest.

This dude had some learning to do about sorcerers if he thought dying wasn't something we were capable of doing. I dropped another anvil on him. This time I was ready for the pain. The crushing lack of light or air or sense of where I was.

A hunch. And a prayer to the Universe that I wasn't totally stupid. That's all I had. My gamble was that the crushing, airless place was the real world. In my experience, only reality could hurt that much.

There was only a second to act. A second to reach for the thread of my own magic. I wasn't even sure I was awake but something answered me, a tendril of fire that I grasped with every panicked ounce of my consciousness.

And I was ready for the cotton-candy scented strands that pulled me back into the dreamland or whatever this hellscape was. I spun my own thread of magic around them, linking us together, forging a pathway between my mind and that of my tormentor.

"Okay asshole," I said. "Show me who you are."

15

It wasn't the hillside but the hospital that appeared around me. I knelt on the floor, a strip of red cloth wound around my left hand and stretched like a rope straight into the white wall. The cotton-candy scent lingered and my hand burned beneath the cloth. I knew without understanding how that the strip was my own magic, a visualization of the hold I had on the sorcerer's spell, and hopefully on him, whoever he was.

A young woman lay in the hospital bed. Helena. Her name slipped into my head. She had red-gold hair that curled in ringlets around her face and wide-set grey-green eyes. Her face was ravaged by pain but she still had a kind of fragile beauty that could have launched a dozen ships if not a thousand.

"Ethan, I want to go home," she said, speaking to someone on the other side of the bed.

"Rest," a man's voice said. "They want one more night for observation, then I'll take you home, I promise."

I rose to my feet. A white man with a tired face and shaggy brown hair sat in the chair. His dress shirt and slacks were rumpled as though he'd spent the night there. Even as I watched his face changed from concern to rage as his watery blue eyes suddenly focused past the woman and onto me. The woman disappeared.

"Hi, Ethan," I said.

"Get out," he snarled. He thrust his hands toward me and a wave of force slammed me into the window.

I yanked on the red cloth, tugging the threads of our interwoven magic. He wasn't going to shake me that easily. The cloth line pulled me through the wall as though it were paper and I stumbled as the tension broke.

I was in a library. Tall shelves lined the room and antique-looking hooded lamps lent a soft, golden glow to the room. I knew this library.

"Enough," Ethan said, materializing out of the shelves.

Stone walls shot up around us, boxing us in. The red cloth fluttered in my hand as the cotton-candy scent faded back.

"That your memory or mine?" I asked.

Anger twisted Ethan's unremarkable face. He really did have a talent.

"You want to see something?" he said. "Let me show you what I'll do to them."

With a wave of his hand, one wall fell and we stood in a cabin. The walls were wood, uninsulated, with heavy denim curtains imperfectly shutting out the daylight. A folding metal table stood in the middle of the room with an unconscious man on it.

Johnny, aka Halfheart. Ethan moved to the table as my vision blurred. I wasn't just seeing now, I felt another heart beating, thoughts not my own flitting like birds at the edge of my consciousness.

I couldn't look away as Ethan began his spell, using his magic to cut and dice at Halfheart's unconscious mind, reaching deep until he found what he wanted. A glittering thread pulsing in time to the beat of the shifter's heart.

"It was an accident the first time," Ethan said. His voice sounded far away again, as though coming down a tunnel. His tone was calm, measured, almost disinterested, but I sensed the rage living underneath. "I thought maybe if I knew how they worked, these animals, I could find a way to harness their healing power. But you cannot make a shifter. They are so far from human even if they walk upright and speak human words. Just look what happens when you take away the beast, when you free the man…" He trailed off.

I knew because I was inside Ethan's mind that he was going to cut that thread. I knew he was going to do it because he could, for all he'd stumbled upon how to silence shifters because of his search for a cure for Helena. He had made Halfheart into a bomb aimed at reaching me because Halfheart knew who I was, but he had severed the wolf from his beast because of who Ethan was. What he was.

"You are the least human thing here," I said as I coiled the tattered red strip of cloth around my left hand.

"I am what I must be to save her. What would you do, Jade?" he said as the table and man faded away, leaving us once again in a bare concrete box. "Or perhaps I should ask what wouldn't you do to save the man you love? I will live forever and Helena will die, wasting away, rotting. What use is all our power if we cannot save the one we love?"

"You didn't destroy Halfheart out of love," I said. My left hand felt like it was melting but I pushed away all thoughts of pain.

"I don't expect someone who loves a beast to understand," Ethan said, his ugly sneer back. "But you do love, that's real, I feel it in you. It fuels you the way it does me, even so. Give me Samir's heart and I swear to leave you in peace. I need his heart. Look at me. See the truth in what I say."

I saw the truth, but perhaps not as he meant me to see it. I saw into the twisted, ugly heart of him, recognizing now as I grew more familiar with the feel of this strange mind-meld that the ugliness that kept shining through was how my own mind perceived what he'd done, who he was.

Ethan thought he loved Helena but it felt like obsession, not love. The fleeting glimpses of memory I caught flashing around us, images that came and went like shadows on the walls while Ethan stared at me, apparently oblivious, these showed me who he was, showed me the pedestal he'd placed his apparently delicate, ill lover on.

He didn't want to protect her. He wanted to defy the world and play god, and so far he had failed.

"Stop." Ethan glared at me. He threw his hands wide and the cotton-candy threads returned strong enough I could feel them again. I snatched at his magic, the cloth in my hand spiraling out into wall beside me.

"Look up," I said as I opened a pit beneath Ethan's feet.

He fell. I yanked on the red cord and hit the wall face-first. Whatever he had done, I was locked inside. He'd closed me off from his mind.

I closed my eyes and took a deep breath. "There is no spoon," I whispered to myself.

Then I channeled my best impression of Kamala Khan and pulled my fist back.

"Embiggen!" My fist as it swelled to many times its normal size as I slammed it into the wall. Once. Twice. A crack appeared. Three. Four. Slam. Slam.

Then the wall crumbled and I was back in the library.

Ethan stood examining a small leather-bound volume. As I watched the shadows flickered and Noah Grey, the Archivist, stepped out into a pool of lamplight.

"Sit down, Ethan Watts," the vampire said. "I believe we can help each other."

Twice more Ethan broke into the memories and twice more I ejected him with extreme cartoonish prejudice until I had seen enough. The third time I let him wall us off again.

Noah Grey wanted Samir's heart. His given reason was that he didn't trust any sorcerer with it. He'd told Ethan the truth, that destroying Samir's heart would bring the apocalypse and end the world as we know it. I had that information independently from sources I trusted far more than the vampire but Ethan seemed to believe him as well. Or not care.

Because what Noah promised the young sorcerer in return was impossible.

"The vampire is lying to you," I said.

"You have Samir's heart," Ethan said. "I've seen glimpses. I can feel it. Show me."

"You aren't fucking listening to me." I slammed my palm against the smooth concrete wall. I was starting to feel sorry for Helena and not just cause her boyfriend was a megalomaniac serial killer. "Noah can't turn anyone into a vampire. No vampire can." Except the mother of all vampires, I added mentally, hoping he wouldn't catch that thought.

"That's bullshit," Ethan said. "How would you know that?"

I saw no reason to not tell him most of the truth there. "Because I met a necromancer who has probably forgotten more about vampires than we'll ever know. He was pretty freaking adamant that no normal vampire can make a new vampire." Skirting dangerously close to the truth but I had a thin hope that if I could get through to Ethan, to show him Noah's lie, he would back down.

Not that he was going to get away. I'd seen too much of his mind now. As much as I dreaded killing anyone, the First maybe excepted, ever again, Ethan wasn't going to stop. Desperation to save Helena might have started his experiments, but it hadn't given him the complete lack of empathy and ethics his torture of shifters displayed. It was an excuse, not a reason.

"That is my problem to deal with," Ethan said. "Even if I believed you, which I do not."

Even as he spoke the words my vision doubled again.

Ethan did believe me. I felt it the way I'd felt the joy in his intention to sever Halfheart's wolf. He believed me and he didn't care. He wanted Samir's heart. To him, if Noah was lying, then the power in Samir's heart would open other potential paths to save Helena. Even if it ended the world.

He'd asked me what I wouldn't do to save the one I loved. Looking deep into Ethan's twisted psyche, I found no answers for myself, only a horrible doppelganger of what I felt for Alek. A love rotted to its core.

All those years of running around, tracking down and eating the hearts of sorcerers and somehow my evil ex had missed this piece of work. Another reason to curse Samir, I decided. Couldn't even count on him to scoop up all the other monsters.

The concrete walls fell away to a snowy field as gunshots rattled in the trees. Samir and I were pressed eye to eye, our lips almost touching. His blood cascaded over my hand as I pushed the Alpha and Omega into his chest. The snow beneath me should have been cold but felt only soft, crunching slightly as our weight shifted.

"Did I ever tell you the story of the scorpion and the frog?" Samir murmured.

I squeezed my left hand, embracing the razorwire feeling of my magic burning there.

"Goodbye, Ethan," I said. I dropped the anvil on us both and all the air and all the light went out and out and out...

Alek

Alek spun in the air, struggling to keep his feet as the magic wrapped around him released him without warning and he slammed back to the unstable earth. He turned in time to see Jade swallowed by the roaring landslide of rock and debris. He flattened his ears and slitted his eyes against the rising dust, ignoring his desperate instinct to leap after her.

The landslide was death for him but not for her. His head knew this. His heart screamed at him to act, to save her. Screamed that he was failing yet another person he loved.

Alek took that rage and sprang up the hillside. Shale slid under his paws and slowed him but he powered toward the trees. A bullet grazed his side. He rolled the pain of that into his anger. His world narrowed to one thought.

Kill.

The first human he reached tried to swing a gun at him but Alek moved with preternatural speed, emerging from the swirling dust and into the waning sunlight like an avenging ghost. Human flesh and cloth were nothing for his teeth. He shook the corpse once and tossed it aside.

Wolves swarmed up the slope now that the worst of the landslide was below them. The humans had too many targets to shoot and Alek found it easy to keep moving. A grey-furred wolf charging up the hill beside Alek howled with pain as a bullet found its side. Alek leaped over the fallen wolf and in three huge strides reached the gunman, showing him no more mercy than he had the last.

Half a dozen human corpses littered the hillside before the gunshots stopped. Alek caught another as he reached the trees. He tore into that human's retreating back, bringing him down as his claws severed the human's spine with a crunch.

Stillness settled slowly over the landscape as the

rockslide found the bottom of the canyon and finished its run. No more humans moved. No more guns fired.

Alek shifted to human, scanning the direction the man he'd just killed had tried to run. The small stand of firs was only a few trees deep. Beyond it the hillside continued to rise. Nothing moved there. No sign of the enemy sorcerer. Alek doubted he was among the fallen.

Jade.

Alek moved as quickly as the unstable, rocky ground would let him. The landslide had carved a deep trench down the hillside in a nearly perfect line, more evidence it wasn't caused by natural means. A huge pile of boulders and gravel and dirt rested below, smaller rocks and debris still shifting and settling. A large fox leapt up onto the shifting pile, sniffing around one of the bigger rocks. Harper was alive.

No sign of Jade.

Bile rose in Alek's throat as he fought the panic wrapping icy fingers around his heart. She was a sorceress, he reminded himself. She was immortal. He hadn't failed her yet.

"Alek?" Aurelio approached him, cutting across the hill as Alek made his way down.

"How many did you lose?" Alek growled. There were fewer wolves than before.

"Three," Aurelio said. His voice was flat, his expression focused.

Alek knew the look. The appearance of a leader who knew there was more fighting to be done. Who knew the grieving had to wait.

"Watch the hill," Alek said. "They might return. Do not trust your eyes."

"Is Jade…?" Aurelio did not finish the question.

"She is under there," Alek said. He ignored Aurelio's raised eyebrows and resumed picking his way down to the canyon floor.

Harper shifted to human and crouched on the pile of stone and dirt as he approached.

"I can't hear her," she said, her green eyes bright with unshed tears. Panic threaded her voice. "I saw her go under but nothing is moving anymore."

"Jade is immortal," Alek said, keeping his voice calm. It helped that Harper was panicking. Alek had always found it easier to stay sane in dangerous or stressful situations if he had someone he needed to care for. It kept his mind from all his failures. From tallying the dead.

He had learned long ago that there was no purpose in dwelling on those who were beyond help, but the knowledge never made the pain less. His heart was still raw from failing Carlos, the man who had helped raise him, the closest Alek had ever had to a father in his life.

He had failed Carlos, but Jade was here, not gone. He just had to get to her.

"Move," he told Harper.

She scrabbled down off the pile of debris. Alek shifted, his senses sharpening as his tiger took over. He started at the leading edge of the pile where the initial cascade had settled and dug his paws into the loose stones and dirt. Sharp edges stung him but he ignored the discomfort as he began to shift the pile, his sensitive nose hunting for any sign of his mate.

Harper, still in human form, started on her own edge. Two wolves joined on the third side. Slowly, rock by rock, handful of earth by handful of earth, Alek, Harper, and the wolves began to move the pile, to disperse it across the floor of the canyon, seeking the woman trapped beneath it. Glancing up as he shook his head to clear the dust from his face, Alek saw wolves crouched along the upper slope. Their bodies were almost invisible among the stones and brush. They kept vigil, facing the way the last gunmen had run, facing the top of the ridge where their assailants had fled.

Alek reached one of the larger boulders and began to dig around it. The way it had settled, he was not sure anyone would be underneath, but the pile was taller than him on his hind legs and he was unwilling to leave a stone unturned.

Live, Jade, he whispered to her in his mind. An image of her bloody, broken body haunted him, drove him to work faster, dig more even though his paws were not designed for it. But there was no choice. He had walked with her willingly into this trap and he would not abandon her now. He would dig her out, make sure she was safe, and then he was going to go find the sorcerer. He would bring Jade the man's heart on a platter after he had torn the rest into pieces smaller than the grit beneath his paws.

The boulder slid a foot and Alek knew he'd dug enough. He moved around to the far side and put his considerable weight against it. It took multiple hard pushes with his body nearly falling into it to get the rock to slide down the side of the pile. It crashed into the brush there and rolled a little way before settling again. One big stone down, more to go. No sign of Jade.

Alek climbed farther up the mound, putting his nose against the loose earth revealed by removing the stone. He caught the faintest scent of blood and a stronger whiff of strawberry shampoo. He gave a coughing roar. *Jade*. He hoped she was beneath him, that perhaps she could hear him. He was coming for her.

He shifted to human and scooped debris away, throwing it as far behind him as he could. Harper climbed up beside him.

"I smell her," Alek said.

Wordlessly Harper started helping him move the stones and dirt. Grit coated them. Sweat ran down Alek's back and face. His arms were scratched and bleeding as he used them to try to move more and more debris. He nearly skidded off the side twice as he dug, loose stone and soil tumbling into the depression he and Harper had made.

"Dig, from that side," Alek growled at the two wolves.

Then the spot they had been digging began to vibrate. Tiny stones rose into the air. The rock beneath his and Harper's knees began to hum.

A huge wolf-like creature appeared in front of them, almost hovering over the rock pile. Her fur was so black it seemed to eat the late afternoon sunlight. Her tail was long and thick like a snow leopard's, her eyes the black of a night sky and full of stars.

"Wolf," Alek said as he felt a pressure on his mind. He recognized Jade's Undying guardian.

Wolf growled, baring her teeth. Her message was clear.

"Move, everyone back," Alek yelled as he scrambled down the rocks. He grabbed at Harper, pulling her with him. He dragged her away from the rockslide.

"But Jade?" Harper said. "Is she doing that? We can't just leave her."

"She's doing something." Alek realized only he could see Wolf.

The giant pile of brush, dirt, and stone hummed louder. Large rocks split and cracked, becoming smaller rocks. Smaller rocks pulverized into grit. Grit turned to a river of dust that lifted and flowed away beneath Wolf's growling, floating body. The air became choked with it, forcing Alek, Harper, and the wolves to crouch in the weak shelter of the brush, their arms protecting their faces.

Then the dust wind settled. Alek squinted at where the rockslide had been. There was no sign of Wolf. Two huge mounds of sand framed a perfect circle plateau of smooth, sandy ground. In the middle of the circle Jade was alive and coughing.

I was ready for the airless, crushing hell this time. I kept hold of my magic even though exhaustion burned through me and my world was darkness and pain. I reminded myself that air was for people who weren't functionally immortal. My lungs disagreed, violently.

A presence manifested right above me, a light in the darkness, though I was sure my eyes were closed. Wolf. I felt her like a tiny sun above me, her warmth telling me where to go. I was facing up, I was sure of that now.

Rock to mud was a spell I'd done before but the sheer weight of stone and dirt on me was too much. Hanging onto consciousness with my body dying around me hurt to the point I had trouble keeping focus on the magic flowing through me. I had to get out. I had to move the mountain. Mud wouldn't be lighter or easier to move off myself.

Sand. I pictured the weight on me being ground to dust and sent power flowing into the rocks. The darkness around me started to hum. My body began to wake up to more than just pressure. Pain like a thousand needles danced along my skin. I clung to the single image of stone into sand and sand into a river flowing off me. I wasn't here, being crushed alive over and over by thousands of pounds of rock and dirt. I was safe in my mental circle, deep within my magic where no pain could reach me.

There is no pain, I kept telling myself. Only the river. Only the power.

Air, fresh and wonderful and cool on my stinging, scraped skin. I gave a final shove with my magic, blowing the sand away from me, clearing my body of grit and weight until I was blissfully unfettered.

For a long moment I lay, gasping in beautiful air, my lungs expanding a ribcage that was trying to tell me it had seen better days. Things were probably broken but I had toes again. I wiggled them and regretted it as leg muscles protested their existence.

Sorcerer. Danger. I made myself find my hands and scrape sand from my eyes.

Then Alek's arms were around me. I heard voices but they were far away. More sand moved from around my head and cloth scraped my face.

"Jade?" Alek's voice. Real Alek this time. I smelled him, sweat and musk and nothing like candy.

"Hi," I croaked. "I'm here."

I was alive. He was alive. It was a start, but we had much to do.

The first thing I checked after I opened my eyes was my talisman. Samir's heart was still in its spot on the D20 and the die was still around my neck, the magically reinforced chain holding up. Harper knelt a few feet away as I did and I caught the look of relief on her face as well.

We retreated into the valley a short ways to where there was enough cover that anyone coming over the ridge would have a hard time shooting at us. Aurelio had lost three of his pack. One was somewhere underneath the sand that had been the rock slide. The other two had been carried down and laid beside the newly created dunes.

My body was trying to heal as quickly as it could. My insides itched, somehow. The shield I'd had up during the worst of the tumble had kept most of my bones from breaking as far as I could tell, but I'd only been unconscious under there for an hour at most. Trapped in my mind by Ethan, it had felt like a lot more time had passed.

The second thing I discovered was that the Alpha and Omega had fallen from its sheath at some point during my ride inside the rock slide. There was no sign of the dagger in the sand. I tried not to panic about it. The knife had a way of magically returning to me like a cursed item. Samir's heart was a tiny gem and it would stay that way for a while even without the blade's assistance. I hoped, anyway.

The third thing was that my phone had survived. It had a crack in the screen but seemed otherwise intact. Small miracles.

"Any sign of your other three?" I asked Aurelio once I'd gotten a sip of water. My backpack had gone the way of sand as well, but Harper had brought a canteen also.

"No," Aurelio said with a dark glance up the hill toward the ridge.

They were either sensibly hiding or had been captured, I guessed. Or killed. Or worse. I tried not to think about that as memories of Ethan's cruelty threatened to rise in my mind.

I sketched out what I had learned as briefly as I could without saying anything about Samir's heart. It was clear to me that the fewer people who knew about it the better, at least for the moment. I told Aurelio that the sorcerer wanted a thing he believed I had so he could trade it to a vampire. It was basically the truth. Mostly.

"So this sorcerer, Ethan, is doing this because he believes the vampire can give immortality to his dying lover?" The incredulous disgust on Aurelio's face mirrored the faces around me. "He severed Halfheart. For this?"

"No, he severed him because he's an evil fuck who hates shifters I guess."

And because he could, which I kept to myself. I pulled the rats nest that was my braid over my shoulder and tried to smooth it. No, even a rat wouldn't have a nest this clogged with grit. Another minute to recover and breathe would have been nice but I knew the next thing I was going to propose would cause a riot.

"Where is he?" Aurelio asked even as his eyes turned back to the side of the canyon.

"Over that ridge," I said. I'd seen as much inside Ethan's mind. There were two cabins still standing there at the termination of an old logging access road.

"There's nothing there, just more rock," he said.

"Illusion."

Alek handed me the canteen again and I took another sip. All I wanted to do was curl up against him forever. Not piss him off. Again.

"He's probably going to run, from what I saw in his mind," I added. "Which is why we have to attack now. I am going to go first and try to break the illusion so you can see where you are going and who to fight."

"No," Alek said, as I had known he would. "You are hurt."

My shoulder was a single throbbing ache and my ribs felt like I'd tried to stop a truck with them but it didn't matter. I didn't want to think about how painful using magic was going to be. I'd been burning that pool low for three days now but I had more to give. There was no choice. Ethan wouldn't stop coming at me.

He wouldn't stop doing evil, awful things under the pretense of saving Helena, either. And I didn't want to even contemplate what he'd do, how much worse he'd become once she died. Which she would, because immortality wasn't, as far as I knew, something you could just conjure up or bargain for.

Harper hadn't said a word since broke out of the rockslide. She stood a short distance away, staring out into nothing as far as I could tell. But at Alek's words she turned and nodded at me as she met my gaze.

"She's right," Harper said. "We have to end this. It's not going to get easier."

Alek made an unhappy noise but he let me hold his arm as I struggled to get my feet under me. I saw his anger and resignation. I wished there was time to tell him what it meant to me that he was here, fighting beside me, keeping me safe. I wished I had the words to let him know that he was protecting me, perhaps not as well physically as he might wish, but that his willingness to follow me into almost certain doom over and over was its own kind of power. Its own kind of saving.

I wanted to tell him that he'd already saved me long ago by showing me that fighting was better than running. That being with those we love was worth the risks of losing them. All I could do was stare into his unhappy blue eyes and try to show him what I felt.

His expression softened and he gave me a slight nod. I didn't have the words or the time, but love has its own mindreading powers.

"All right," I said aloud. I leaned more heavily on Alek's arm than I wanted to as I stood. "Here's the plan."

When I'm rested and at full power, flying, at least the only way I'd ever figured out how to fly in the real world, is terrifying and magic-consuming like crazy.

I was not rested. I was more scraping out the jam jar hoping there'd be enough for a meal level of power. But Death from Above was pretty much my entire plan. Nobody ever looks up.

Rising above the edge of the canyon, the plateau up there stretched out in apparent emptiness. I knew what it had looked like in Ethan's mind, however, and was able to see details of rocks and a few trees that he hadn't covered in illusion. There was a lone pine standing tall among clumps of grass and a few scattered boulders. It was a strong illusion. Ethan, from what I'd seen in his mind, like to plan. He liked to prepare.

I flew high above the pine. The cabins were near that tree, I was sure of it. Beyond I saw the old logging path snaking into more trees that formed a dark shadow on the quickly dimming landscape as the sun settled ever lower in the sky. My magic was liquid fire in my blood and I fed it every fear I had, every hope, every ounce of rage and pain until my body felt incandescent and my mind a laser focused on what should be below.

One of the worst things to encounter when playing Dungeons & Dragons is anti-magic anything. Dispel Magic is almost as evil as having a rust monster eat your player's equipment. Magic items destroyed or levels lost through level drain are up there in the pantheon of do-not-want. I had no idea if Dispel Magic would work in the real world, but I could cast fireballs so I figured if I could envision it, I could do it. I just hoped I didn't pass out a couple hundred feet above the ground trying to get this spell off.

Power swirled in purple sparks around my hands. I visualized the spell in a cone attack, feeding more and more magic into it as the sparks spread out like a carpet beneath me. I hoped I'd given Alek and Aurelio and the pack enough time to reach the edge of the ridge but I didn't dare try to turn and look. It was taking all my concentration to keep hovering here while I worked the second spell.

One last deep breath that caught on my injured ribs and I released the cone, pushing the carpet of sparks down. My body followed them as I dropped from the sky like a bird of prey. The ground reached toward me with far too much speed and I shoved against it with more magic to slow myself.

The sparks hit the illusion and a boom echoed across the canyon. For a moment I had double vision. Rocks and a lone tree. Grasses and sage brush rippling in the breeze giving way to a bare area where the ground was churned up by tires and human feet. Two wooden cabins and the half-collapsed remains of a third appeared, wavered, then solidified.

Half a dozen men in grey and tan fatigues were putting things into two Jeeps parked near a beat-up old truck. As I descended from the sky they started shouting. Wolves broke from the brush around them and I heard Alek's challenging roar. The men went for their guns.

A rock the size of my head flew at me as I landed, appearing from nowhere. I slammed a shield in place and the rock fizzled on it.

Illusion again.

Ethan ran out of the nearest cabin, a gun in one hand. He threw up his other hand and a wall of stone cut me off from him.

Idiot had brought illusions and a gun to a mage fight. He wasn't inside my head anymore. We were in the real world now and he was about to find out what kind of sorceress I was. Illusions, mind-magic, trickery, those were his domain. Mine was the liberal and excessive expenditure of awesome destructive power and I was done with his shit.

Purple sparks formed shields around my fists as I charged the wall. I punched my way right through the illusion, ignoring my mind screaming at me that this was solid and going to hurt me. Cotton-candy magic gummed my senses. I added that to Ethan's list of sins. I had *liked* cotton-candy.

Ethan shot at me but he clearly hadn't practiced much with a gun. Hitting a moving target in a stressful situation is difficult even for the well-trained. From how he dropped the large revolver on the recoil, Ethan was far from trained. I charged toward him and sent my power out like tentacles. He tried to shield himself but I smashed through his magic like it was made of the spun sugar it smelled like. Out of the corner of my eye I saw Alek's white tiger tear a man's head clear of his body.

Ethan collapsed to his knees as my magic entangled him. He tried to reach for the gun but I made my hands into fists, tightening the tentacles binding him.

"Stop, I yield," he cried out.

"No shit," I said. I kept the bonds tight as I stalked toward him, watching my periphery for other attackers.

From the cabin Ethan hadn't come out of, a wolf started howling. Aurelio charged past in his wolf form, breaking down the cabin's door with a single powerful slam of his body.

"I left them alive. They are fine," Ethan said, talking fast as he glanced behind to where the huge black wolf had disappeared. The howling stopped.

I wondered if Ethan thought that would save him. Aurelio, in human form, emerged from the cabin again.

"Keys?" he growled, looking at Ethan with murder in his dark face.

"Larry had them," the sorcerer said with an audible gulp. "Big guy, red hair." He looked around.

I couldn't see behind me but I could guess, from the lack of gunfire or any noise at all, that there were only corpses left of Ethan's men. A big brown and white wolf trotted past with a keychain dangling from its mouth. Aurelio took the keys and went back into the cabin.

Fatigue put red stars into my vision and my magic ebbed slightly, reminding me I was running out of time before I really had to rest. I had to deal with Ethan.

Alek prowled into the cabin Ethan had been in but emerged moments later. He shifted to human.

"Empty," he said.

Something about that didn't sit right with me. I watched Ethan's face as relief flickered across it before he could school himself back to glaring at me.

"More tricks?" I said to him. "Where's Helena?" He wouldn't leave her somewhere, I felt that deep in my aching bones.

Ethan shook his head, the only movement he could manage with my magic wrapped around him like a boa constrictor.

"Watch the cabin door, be careful," I said to Alek.

He nodded and moved to the side of the door where he would be out of sight, and hard to attack or shoot. Not that the sick woman I'd met in Ethan's memories was likely to put up much of a challenge. I was glad she was hiding. We'd have to deal with her, too, but it was better perhaps that she not see what came next.

Aurelio emerged from the cabin followed by a limping white wolf. A large reddish-brown wolf and a smaller brown wolf followed. Raw lines marred the wolves' necks where they had been chained up. They snarled but Aurelio held up a hand.

"She's dealing with him," he said as he met my gaze. There was anger and death in his eyes and I knew there was only one kind of justice he would accept.

I took a couple shallow breaths and walked up to Ethan. His flat blue eyes glared up at me.

"I'll leave," he said. "We'll go far away. I promise."

Even if I had believed him, which I did not, I knew in my broken heart that I couldn't let him go. Ethan wouldn't stop trying to save Helena. He wouldn't stop hurting people, either, in his quest for power. He mistook it for a kind of strength and he loved feeling strong. Helena's illness, her mortality, they made him helpless and he would rage and destroy whatever he had to in order to try to run from that feeling.

And I knew the truth of his love, too. For inside his mind, through the memories I'd touched, I had seen how he perceived love. How he looked at Helena. She was beautiful and precious to him, but like a pet or a prized doll. I had seen nothing of who *she* was as a person. Because her personhood wasn't important to Ethan. There was no give and take, no partnership in their relationship. She was a shiny thing to him, a reflection of his own self-image. He was angry at the world for breaking his toy. He wanted her to go on living so he could keep what he thought of as his.

"You won't," I said.

I pushed magic around my hand again, forming violet claws at the end of my fingers. This was never going to get easier. Which was a relief, in some ways. I didn't want this to ever be easy. I was not Samir and I would fight to the bitter end to never become him.

"No!" Ethan cried out. "Please. You don't understand. I tried to show you. I have to save her. But you don't get it do you? You don't really love."

He was wrong, wrong in ways he'd never understand. Love meant trust. Trusting others enough to let them be themselves and knowing they would set you free in return. Love was inherently surrender, sacrifice without expectation. No one, no matter how powerful, could control the fate of another. We could only do what we were capable of and hope it was enough.

"You asked me what I wouldn't do to save the ones I love," I whispered as I bent close to him. "You assumed I didn't already know. But I do."

Because I did. I'd stood in a snow-packed clearing covered in the blood of everyone I cared most about in the world. I'd knelt with all the power of the ley lines beneath Wylde and the River of No Return running through my blood and watched my own heart beat in Samir's hand. I would carry with me forever the image of Alek's chest open and gushing, his face burned, the light fading from his eyes even as he reached for me one. Last. Time.

And I'd made a decision that day. For love. I'd taken the power that could have ended Samir and I'd rent the very fabric of time and space. I'd turned back what had been our futures and remade the world, possibly breaking things that I couldn't even begin to comprehend.

Ethan didn't know this. He wouldn't understand it.

His quest for a cure for Helena, for immortality for her was born from his ultimate desire to be powerful, to fight the helplessness he felt at forces in the world he couldn't control. His vision was as small and cruel as he was.

He would never stop hurting those he considered weaker. If Helena was cured, or, more likely, when she died, he would go on as he had been. Ethan had tried to crack into my mind and in so doing shone a light into himself. I guess the abyss really does stare back.

"Go to hell," he said.

I slammed my hand into his chest, my magic claws tearing through flesh and bone to the heart beneath. I pulled it free and brought it to my lips. One bite. That's all it took. Ethan crumped as I swallowed the chunk of wet, warm flesh.

Nope. Never got easier. Or less gross. Ethan's power had been nearly drained as well and the drops that fell into my own tapped-out well were pathetic. It would recover with time, as would I. I carefully sealed off the rush of memories that flooded through my mind. I'd have to deal with those, too, at some point. And it was only a matter of time before I was faced with ghost-Ethan in my head.

But not today. I wanted a shower and a milkshake the size of a car and about three days of uninterrupted sleep. In that order but I wasn't about to be picky.

"No!" Helena burst from the cabin. Alek grabbed her and she struggled against him.

The woman in Ethan's memory had been frail, clearly sick but still beautiful. The woman in Alek's arm digging her fingers into his flesh was a shadow of that. Her grey-green eyes were sunken, buried by dark puffy circles. Her hair was pulled back in a ponytail, its red-gold color dull even in the sunlight. Her bones were like sticks beneath skin stretched and thin as tissue paper. Memory-Helena had looked like a doll. This Helena looked like a bad papier-mâché reconstruction of that doll.

"Let her go," I said to Alek. She was a sick human and for all that Ethan was evil and she had probably been complicit in that, I had no intention of killing her. Life would do that soon enough.

I didn't even look to where Harper hovered nearby. She was probably on the side of "kill everyone who might be an enemy" but I was tired.

"You killed him?" Helena said as she staggered toward.

"He was evil," I said as I dropped the remains of his heart onto the ground. I could only imagine how I looked. Covered in grit and blood, my hair a ragged nest. I'm sure I sounded really convincing but I had no words to explain to her what I'd seen in Ethan's mind. Likely she knew in her heart what he was, how he truly perceived her. This woman was going to need a lot of therapy. I suppressed the giggle that rose unbidden. I was definitely reaching my limits.

She fell to her knees beside him, blood soaking into her white dress as she grabbed at Ethan's hand.

"I was going to be a vampire," she said. She dropped his lifeless hand and stared at the blood pooling around her knees.

"You weren't," I said. "The vampire lied. He was using you both."

Helena nodded slowly. She seemed strangely calm. I had expected tears or screaming. I mean, either or both would be rational responses to someone ripping out your lover's heart, I imagined. I had a feeling that being with Ethan might have done terrible things to her psyche already. A memory threatened, not one of mine, and I quickly threw a silver circle around it in my head. I did not want to know. Nope.

"Are you going to kill me?" Her gaze rose from the blood to search my face.

"No," I said as gently as I could manage. "He was the threat, not you." I hoped. She didn't look like she could manage to punch out a cricket, but I took a short step back anyway before motioning to Alek. "Let's put her in a vehicle I guess. We'll drop you somewhere," I added for Helena's sake.

She took advantage of my distraction and grabbed the gun beside Ethan. Alek lunged for her at the same time I did.

We were both too late. She turned the barrel toward her face and pulled the trigger even as my hands closed on her arms.

There was no plumbing in the cabins but Ethan's people had been well supplied and Alek found enough water and a towel to clean the worst of the blood and grime from me. Aurelio's pack had shifted to human to do the work of moving the bodies.

"Take her home," he told Alek as I staggered to my feet. "We'll bury them and clean all this up."

I was surprised I was still conscious but there was more to do if we were not going to leave a murder field behind.

"Thank you," Alek said.

"I would argue, but I won't," I said. "I'm sorry about your people." I didn't even know their names, I realized, but was too exhausted to ask.

"It would have been worse without you," he said. "Bird, Snowdrop, and Always Singing would be dead. Or worse."

Ethan had definitely intended worse, but I didn't tell him that.

"You coming?" I said instead to Harper. She was hovering silently a few feet away.

"No," she said. Then she burst forward and wrapped her arms around me.

It hurt like hell but I returned the hug and let her cling, leaning into her strong body and fighting the sudden tears that blurred my vision.

"I'm sorry," she said. "I'm not mad anymore. I know you just want to protect us."

"Hey, furball, it's okay," I murmured into her hair. I pulled back a little so I could look her in the eye. "You were right. I should have told you. When we get back, when Ezee is back, we're going to talk. No more secrets. It's not always easy for me to explain but I'm going to try, okay?"

Harper nodded. "I'm glad you aren't dead."

"Me, too." I didn't mention how much having her arms around my damaged ribs was killing me. Or that

ANNIE BELLET

I was leaning on her partially because I was maybe minutes from passing the fuck out. "You coming? Alek found keys to the cars. We don't have to hike back."

"No," Harper said, letting me go. I tried not to stagger, or sigh with relief. "I'm going to stay and help out, then go back with Softpaw's pack. I could use the thinking time, you know?"

"Yeah, I know. See you tomorrow?" I wrapped a hand around my talisman, feeling Samir's heart still there, a tiny reminder of the problems ahead of us.

Alek picked me up and I didn't even have the energy to protest. I rested my head against his chest until he set me down in the passenger side of the old truck.

"Not a jeep? They look nicer," I said.

"Leg room," Alek replied as he buckled me in and then closed the door.

It was easy to forget sometimes that he was half a foot or more taller than most people. He always seemed to manage in my regular-people-sized car, though I usually did the driving.

"You know how to get out of here?" Alek asked me as he started the engine.

"Follow the logging path," I said. I closed my eyes and found the route in Ethan's memories, deftly dodging anything except the information I wanted. It was a sign of how many people I'd eaten I guess that I could do that even when exhausted. I pushed that grim thought away and pulled out my phone.

I'd left a message for Lara and for Levi before we'd come out here but I imagined they were worried. My phone turned on after an agonizing moment. The screen crack appeared superficial as I was able to swipe the unlock code. No bars, no service. "Hey we aren't all dead" texts would have to wait.

The road was overgrown and the ride was a mess of bumps and bounces. It was full dark by the time we reached a real road and I'd added about twenty bruises to my collection. Alek guided the truck onto the proper asphalt and I sagged in the seat.

"Sleep, Jade," he said, his teeth flashing white in the blue light from the dashboard. "I can take us home from here."

There were only so many roads into Wylde that I knew he was right.

"I'm almost afraid to rest," I said. "What's waiting for us?" I wanted to strangle myself for confessing the fears aloud but they were rattling around in my head, fueled by my own tiredness.

"Whatever is waiting, we'll face it." Alek's voice was soft, gentle. Confident.

"You do, you know," I said, closing my eyes. I loosened my seat belt so I could lay across the bench seat and rest my aching cheek on his thigh. "Protect me, I mean. You keep me safe."

"I will always keep you safe," Alek said, his voice suspiciously rough. I felt him take a very deep breath.

"He asked me what I would do to save you," I said. My body felt light, the pain fading back as unconsciousness crept over me like a familiar blanket. "Everything. He didn't understand but I do. Because I did it for you." I knew I wasn't making sense but the fog in my mind refused to form better words.

I'd changed the world for the people I'd loved. I'd change it again if I had to. I hoped, as I drifted into the darkness, that my found family, my mate, that they understood.

"I know, kitten. I remember," came the softly spoken words that sang me to sleep.

If you want to be notified when Annie Bellet's next novel or collection is released, please sign up for the mailing list by going to: http://tinyurl.com/anniebellet Your email address will never be shared and you can unsubscribe at any time. Want to find more Twenty-Sided Sorceress books? Go here:

http://anniebellet.com/series/twenty-sided-sorceress/ for links and more information.

Word-of-mouth and reviews are vital for any author to succeed. If you enjoyed the book, please tell your friends and consider leaving a review wherever you purchased it. Even a few lines sharing your thoughts on this story would be extremely helpful for other readers. Thank you!

Also by Annie Bellet

The Gryphonpike Chronicles:
Witch Hunt
Twice Drowned Dragon
A Stone's Throw
Dead of Knight
The Barrows (Omnibus Vol.1)
Brood Mother
Into the North

Chwedl Duology:
A Heart in Sun and Shadow
The Raven King (Winter 2020)

Pyrrh Considerable Crimes Division Series:
Avarice
Wrath (Fall 2019)

Short Story Collections:
Till Human Voices Wake Us
Dusk and Shiver
Forgotten Tigers and Other Stories

About the Author

Annie Bellet lives and writes in the Netherlands. She is the *USA Today* bestselling author of the *Gryphonpike Chronicles* and the *Twenty-Sided Sorceress* series. Follow her at her website at www.anniebellet.com

Made in the USA
Columbia, SC
08 July 2021

41580784R00136